Born and bred in Abruzzo, **Donatella Di Pietrantonio** lives in Penne, where she practices as a paediatric dentist. Her short fiction has been published by *Granta* Italy, and her novel, *Bella mia*, was nominated f Brancati Prize. Her first noveished in the UK by Calisi Presel, won the Campiello Prize i

Ann Goldstein has translated into English all of Elena Ferrante's books, including the *New York Times* bestseller, *The Story of the Lost Child*, which was shortlisted for the MAN Booker International Prize. She has been honoured with a Guggenheim Fellowship and is a recipient of the PEN Renato Poggioli Translation Award. She lives in New York.

A GIRL RETURNED

Donatella Di Pietrantonio

A GIRL RETURNED

*Translated from the Italian
by Ann Goldstein*

Europa
editions

Europa Editions
8 Blackstock Mews
London N4 2BT
www.europaeditions.co.uk

Translation by Ann Goldstein
Original title: *L'Arminuta*
Translation copyright © 2019 by Europa Editions

A catalogue record for this title is available from the British Library
ISBN 978-1-78770-265-3

Di Pietrantonio, Donatella
A Girl Returned

Book design by Emanuele Ragnisco
www.mekkanografici.com

Cover illustration by Elisa Talentino

Prepress by Grafica Punto Print – Roma

Printed and bound in Great Britain by Clays Ltd, Elcograf S.p.A.

For Piergiorgio, who was here for such a short time

Even today, in a way, I'm still in that childhood summer:
my soul ceaselessly spins and pulses around it,
like an insect around a blinding light.
—ELSA MORANTE, *Lies and Sorcery*

A GIRL RETURNED

1.

I was thirteen, yet I didn't know my other mother. I struggled up the stairs to her apartment with an unwieldy suitcase and a bag of jumbled shoes. On the landing I was greeted by the smell of recent frying and a wait. The door wouldn't open: someone was shaking it wordlessly on the inside and fussing with the lock. I watched a spider wriggle in the empty space, hanging at the end of its thread.

There was a metallic click, and a girl with loose braids that hadn't been done for several days appeared. She was my sister, but I had never seen her. She opened the door wide so I could come in, keeping her sharp eyes on me. We looked like each other then, more than we do as adults.

2.

The woman who had conceived me didn't get up from the chair. The child she held in her arms was sucking his thumb on one side of his mouth—maybe a tooth was coming in. Both of them looked at me, and he stopped his monotonous crying. I didn't know I had such a little brother.

"You're here," she said. "Put down your things."

I lowered my eyes to the smell of shoes that wafted from the bag if I moved it even slightly. From behind the closed door of the room at the back came a tense, sonorous snoring. The baby started whining again and turned to the breast, dripping saliva on the sweaty, faded cotton flowers.

"Why don't you close the door?" the mother curtly asked the girl, who hadn't moved.

"Aren't the people who brought her coming up?" she objected, indicating me with her pointy chin.

My uncle, as I was supposed to learn to call him, entered just then, panting after the stairs. In the heat of the summer afternoon he was holding with two fingers the hanger of a new coat, my size.

"Your wife didn't come?" my first mother asked, raising her voice to cover the wailing in her arms that grew louder and louder.

"She can't get out of bed," he answered, turning his head. "Yesterday I went to buy some things, for winter, too," and he showed her the label bearing the name of the coat's maker.

I moved toward the open window and put down the bags.

In the distance a loud din, like rocks being unloaded from a truck.

The woman decided to offer the guest coffee; the smell, she said, would wake her husband. She moved from the bare dining room to the kitchen, after putting the child in the playpen to cry. He tried to pull himself up holding onto the netting, just next to a hole that had been crudely repaired with a tangle of string. When I approached, he cried louder, upset. His everyday sister lifted him out with an effort and put him down on the tile floor. He crawled toward the voices in the kitchen. Her dark look shifted from her brother to me, remaining low. It scorched the gilt buckles of my new shoes, moved up along the blue pleats of the dress, still rigid from the store. Behind her a fly buzzed in midair, now and then flinging itself at the wall, in search of a way out.

"Did that man get this dress for you, too?" she asked softly.

"He got it for me yesterday, just to come back here."

"But what's he to you?" she asked, curious.

"A distant uncle. I lived with him and his wife till today."

"Then who is your mamma?" she asked, discouraged.

"I have two. One is your mother."

"Sometimes she talked about it, about an older sister, but I don't much believe her."

Suddenly she grabbed the sleeve of my dress with eager fingers.

"Pretty soon it won't fit you anymore. Next year you can hand it down to me, be careful you don't ruin it."

The father came out of the bedroom, shoeless, yawning, bare-chested. Noticing me as he followed the aroma of the coffee, he introduced himself.

"You're here," he said, like his wife.

The words coming from the kitchen were few and muffled, the spoons were no longer tinkling. When I heard the sound of the chairs shifting, I was afraid; my throat tightened. My uncle came over to say goodbye, with a hurried pat on the cheek.

"Be good," he said.

"I left a book in the car, I'm coming down to get it," and I followed him down the stairs.

With the excuse of looking in the glove compartment, I got in the car. I closed the door and pressed the lock.

"What are you doing?" he asked, already in the driver's seat.

"I'm going home with you, I won't be any trouble. Mamma's sick, she needs my help. I'm not staying here, I don't know those people up there."

"Let's not start again, try to be reasonable. Your real parents are expecting you and they'll love you. It'll be fun to live in a house full of kids." He breathed in my face the coffee he'd just drunk, mingled with the odor of his gums.

"I want to live in my house, with you. If I did something wrong tell me, and I won't do it again. Don't leave me here."

"I'm sorry, but we can't keep you anymore, we've already explained it. Now please stop this nonsense and get out," he concluded, staring straight ahead at nothing. Under his beard, unshaved for several days, the muscles of his jaw were pulsing the way they sometimes did when he was about to get angry.

I disobeyed, continuing to resist. Then he punched the steering wheel and got out, intending to pull me out of the small space in front of the seat that I had squeezed myself into, trembling. He opened the door with the key and grabbed me by the arm; the shoulder seam of the dress he had bought me came unstitched in one place. In his grip I no longer recognized the hand of the taciturn father I'd lived with until that morning.

I remained on the asphalt with the tire marks in the big, empty square. The air smelled of burning rubber. When I raised my head, someone from the family that was mine against my will was looking down from the second-floor windows.

He returned half an hour later. I heard a knock and then his voice on the landing. I forgave him instantly and picked up my bags with a rush of joy, but when I reached the door his footsteps were already echoing at the bottom of the stairs. My sister was holding a container of vanilla ice cream, my favorite flavor. He had come for that, not to take me away. The others ate it, on that August afternoon in 1975.

4.

Toward evening the older boys came home: one greeted me with a whistle, another didn't even notice me. They rushed into the kitchen, elbowing one another to grab places at the table, where the mother was serving dinner. The plates were filled amid splashes of sauce: only a spongy meatball in a little sauce reached my corner. It was colorless inside, made with stale bread and a few bits of meat. We ate bready meatballs with more bread dipped in the sauce to fill our stomachs. After a few days I would learn to compete for food and stay focused on my plate to defend it from aerial fork raids. But that night I lost the little that the mother's hand had added to my scant ration.

My first parents didn't recall until after dinner that there wasn't a bed for me in the house.

"Tonight you can sleep with your sister, you're both thin," the father said. "Tomorrow we'll see."

"For us both to fit, we have to lie opposite, head to toe," Adriana explained to me. "But we can wash our feet now," she reassured me.

We soaked them in the same basin, and she spent a long time getting out the dirt between her toes.

"Look how black the water is," she laughed. "That's mine, yours were already clean."

She dug up a pillow for me, and we went into the room without turning on the light: the boys were breathing as if asleep, and the sweat smell of adolescents was strong. We settled ourselves head to foot, whispering. The mattress, stuffed with sheep's wool, was soft and shapeless from use, and I sank toward the center. It gave off the ammonia smell of pee, which saturated it, a new and repellent odor to me. The mosquitoes were looking for blood and I would have liked to cover myself with the sheet, but in her sleep Adriana had pulled it in the opposite direction.

A sudden jolt of her body—maybe she was dreaming of falling. Gently I moved her foot and leaned my cheek against the sole, fresh with cheap soap. For most of the night I stayed against the rough skin, moving whenever she moved her legs. With my fingers I felt the uneven edges of her broken nails. There were some clippers in my bag, in the morning I could give them to her.

The last quarter of the moon peeked in through the open window and traveled across it. The trail of stars remained, along with the minimum good fortune that the sky was clear of houses in that direction.

Tomorrow we'll see, the father had said, but then he forgot. I didn't ask him, nor did Adriana. Every night she lent me the sole of her foot to hold against my cheek. I had nothing else, in that darkness inhabited by breath.

A wet warmth spread under my ribs and hip. I sat up with a start and touched between my legs: it was dry. Adriana shifted in the darkness, but continued to lie there. Wedged into the corner, she resumed or went on sleeping, as if she were used to it. After a while I lay down, too, making myself as small as I could. We were two bodies around the wet spot.

Slowly the odor vanished, rising only now and again. Near dawn, one of the boys, I couldn't tell which, began moving rhythmically, faster and faster, for several minutes, moaning.

In the morning Adriana woke up and didn't move, with her head on the pillow and her eyes open. Then she looked at me a moment, without saying anything. The mother came to call her with the child in her arms. She sniffed the air.

"You've wet yourself again, good girl. We make a bad show right away."

"It wasn't me," Adriana answered, turning toward the wall.

"Yes, maybe it was your sister, with the upbringing she's had. Hurry up, it's already late," and they went into the kitchen.

I wasn't prepared to follow them, and then I lost the ability to move. I stood there, lacking even the courage to go to the bathroom. One brother sat on the bed, legs spread. Between yawns he weighed his bulging underpants with one hand. When he noticed me in the room, he began observing me, wrinkling his brow. He paused on my breasts, covered only by the T-shirt I was wearing in place of pajamas, in that heat. Instinctively I crossed my arms over the encumbrance that had only recently grown there, while sweat surfaced in my armpits.

"You slept here, too?" he asked in the voice of a man not yet adult.

I answered yes, embarrassed, while he continued to examine me shamelessly.

"You're fifteen?"

"No, I'm not even fourteen."

"But you look fifteen, maybe more. You developed fast," he concluded.

"How old are you?" I asked, out of politeness.

"I'm almost eighteen, I'm the oldest. I already go to work, but not today."

"Why?"

"The boss doesn't need me today. He calls when he needs me."

"What do you do?"

"Laborer."

"And school?"

"Oh yeah, school! I quit in the second year of middle school, anyhow they failed me."

I saw the muscles molded by the work, the strong shoulders. A chestnut spray rose on his sunburned chest and, higher, over his face. He, too, must have grown up quickly. When he stretched I smelled an adult odor, not unpleasant. A scar in the shape of a fish bone decorated his left temple, maybe an old wound that had been poorly sutured.

We didn't say anything else, again he was looking at my body. From time to time he adjusted his penis with his hand, to a less awkward position. I wanted to get dressed, but I hadn't unpacked my suitcase the day before, and it was still on the other side of the room: I would have had to take some steps with my back to him to go and get it. I waited for something to happen. His gaze slowly descended from my cotton-covered hips to my bare legs, to my contracted feet. I wouldn't turn.

The mother came in and told him to hurry up, a neighbor was looking for help with a job in the countryside. In exchange he would give him some crates of ripe tomatoes, for making sauce.

"Go with your sister to get the milk if you want breakfast," she then ordered me. She tried to soften her tone, but by the end of the sentence she'd gone back to the usual.

In the other room the baby had crawled over to my bag of shoes and scattered them all around. He was biting one, his mouth looking as if he'd tasted something bitter. Adriana was already cleaning the beans for lunch, kneeling on a chair against the kitchen table.

"Look how you're wasting all the good part." The complaint reached her punctually.

She paid no attention.

"Go wash up, then we'll go and get some milk, I'm hungry," she said to me.

I was the last to use the bathroom. The boys had splashed water on the floor and had walked in it, imprints of bare feet and soles of shoes were superimposed on one another. At my house I'd never seen the tiles such a mess. I slipped, but without hurting myself, like a ballerina. Certainly I would not go back to dancing school in the fall, or swimming lessons.

I remember one of those mornings in the beginning, when a pale light coming through the windows proclaimed a storm that would break later, as had happened the other days. There was a strange quiet; Adriana had gone with the baby to visit the widow who lived on the ground floor, and the boys were all out. I was alone in the house with the mother.

"Pluck the chicken," she ordered me, handing me the dead bird she was holding by the claws, its head dangling. Someone must have brought it up to her; I'd heard some conversation on the landing and, at the end, her thanks. "Then gut it."

"What? I don't understand."

"You're going to eat it like that? You have to get rid of the feathers, no? Then you cut it up and throw away the guts," she explained, slightly shaking the arm extended toward me.

I took a step back and averted my eyes.

"I can't, it scares me. I can do the cleaning."

She looked at me without saying anything else. She slammed the carcass on the sink counter with a muffled thud, and began furiously pulling out the feathers.

"The only chickens that one's seen are cooked," I heard her muttering between her teeth.

I got busy cleaning, that wasn't difficult. Other domestic tasks I didn't know how to do, I wasn't used to them. I spent a long time with a sponge scrubbing the chalk stain that stretched along the bottom of the tub, then I opened the tap to fill it. With cold water—no hot came out, and I didn't want to ask. Now and then from the kitchen came the sound of bones being chopped, while I went on sweating over the dirty bathroom fixtures. Finally I closed the door from the inside with the metal hook, and immersed myself. When I reached out my hand toward the soap on the edge, I felt I was about to die. The blood rushed out of my head, my arms, my chest, and left them freezing. Seconds remained for two necessities: open the drain and ask for help. I didn't know how to get the attention of the woman out there, I couldn't call her mamma. In place of the sequence "m" and "a" I vomited lumps of lactic acid into the water that was draining. I no longer even remembered her name, if I had wanted to call it. So I yelled and then I fainted.

I don't know how much time had passed when the dry odor of Adriana's pee woke me. I was lying naked on the bed, with a towel over me. On the floor beside me was an empty glass that must have contained sugar dissolved in water, the cure the mother used for every ailment. Later she looked in at the door of the room.

"If you start feeling sick can't you say so right away, instead of waiting for the worst?" she asked, chewing something.

"I'm sorry, I thought it would pass," I answered without looking at her.

I never called to her, not for years. From the moment I was given back to her, the word "mamma" had stuck in my throat like a frog that wouldn't jump out. If I had to speak to her urgently, I tried to get her attention in various ways. Sometimes, if I was holding the baby, I pinched his legs to make him cry. Then she would turn in our direction and I spoke to her.

For a long time I forgot those small tortures inflicted on my brother, and only now, when he's in his twenties, I happened to remember them. I was sitting next to him on a bench, in the place where he lives, and I noticed a bruise on his skin like the ones I used to leave. This time it was the corner of some piece of furniture that had got him.

At dinner they were all excited about the novelty of the chicken; Adriana asked if it was Christmas in summer. I was torn between hunger and disgust at having seen it gutted, its insides hanging in the sink, amid the dirty breakfast cups.

"A thigh for Papa and one for the girl who fainted today," the mother decided. But the other pieces were much smaller, and bony, after the breast had been set aside for the next day. The one they called Sergio immediately rebelled.

"If she's sick she should eat broth, not the thigh," he protested. "It should be mine, today I helped that woman upstairs move and you took the money I earned."

"Plus it was her fault you busted the bathroom door," another one broke in, shaking his index finger at me. "All she does is make trouble, can't you give her back to the people who had her before?"

With a clap on the head the father pushed him down in his chair and silenced him.

"I'm not hungry anymore," I said to Adriana and escaped into the bedroom. She joined me soon afterward, with a slice of bread and oil. She had cleaned up and changed, and was wearing a skirt that was too small.

"Hurry up, as soon as you finish get dressed so we can go to the festival." She stuck the plate under my nose.

"What festival?"

"The patron saint—didn't you hear the band? And the singers are starting right now, up in the square. But we're not going there, Vincenzo will take us to the rides," she whispered.

Less than half an hour later the fish bone on Vincenzo's temple was shining under the street lights where the road widened and the Gypsies were camped. He was the only one of the boys who hadn't attacked me in the argument about the chicken thigh, and he hadn't invited his brothers to come, only Adriana and me. He counted the change he'd scraped together somehow or other, and lingered a while with the ticket-taker: it was clear that they were friendly, maybe from earlier festivals. They smoked together, seemed the same age, and had the same dark skin. The Gypsy took the money for the first rides, then let us go on free.

I had never been on the chair swing ride, my mother said it was too dangerous, and the son of a friend of hers had crushed his thumb on the bumper cars. Adriana, already expert, helped me get up in the seat and closed the safety bar.

"Hold tight to the chains," she urged before sitting in front of me.

I flew between her and Vincenzo—they put me in the middle so I wouldn't be scared. At the highest point I felt a kind of happiness: what had happened to me in the past days stayed on the ground, like a heavy fog. I flew above it and could even forget it, for a while. Suddenly, after a few trial rounds, I felt a foot giving me a push from behind and a voice said: "Grab this tail!" But I reached out timidly, I didn't have the confidence to let go of the chain.

"Reach your hand out, miss, nothin's gonna happen," he incited me, then pushed me harder. On the third try I stretched into the void and felt something hairy beat against my open palm. I squeezed it as hard as I could. I'd won the fox tail and Vincenzo's elation.

The chairs slowed in their clanking circular course and gradually stopped. I got out, took a few involuntary and unsteady steps. Shivers went up and down my arms, but not from cold—after the daily storms the heat returned immediately. He came over and looked silently into my eyes, his sparkled. I had been brave. I straightened my dress, rumpled by the wind. He lighted a cigarette and blew the first puff of smoke in my face.

When we were almost home, Vincenzo gave us his key. He had forgotten something at the rides, we could leave the door partly open for him. But he was late coming home, while I couldn't sleep, still excited by my flight. On the other side of the wall, in the parents' room, a rhythmic squeaking, then nothing. Hours passed, and my legs were fidgety; I hit Adriana's face with one foot. Later, when the wetness arrived as usual, I got up and went to Vincenzo's bed, which was still empty. Moving around I found the odors of the different parts of his body, armpits, mouth, genitals. I imagined him in front of his Gypsy friend's caravan as they chatted past the smoke of their cigarettes. I fell asleep like that, toward dawn.

He showed up at lunch, his work pants stained with solid splotches of cement. No one seemed to have noticed his nighttime absence. His parents merely exchanged a look as he approached the table.

His father struck him coldly, without a word. Vincenzo lost his balance, and as he fell one hand landed in the plate of pasta, its sauce made from the tomatoes he had earned, working in the countryside in the days before. He huddled on the floor in self-defense and, eyes closed, waited for the father to finish. When the man's feet moved away, he rolled a little distance and remained there, supine, recovering on the cool floor.

"Eat, the rest of you," the mother said, with the baby in her arms. He hadn't cried during the commotion, as if he were used to it. The boys obeyed instantly, Adriana somewhat reluctantly, delaying to clean up the tablecloth. Only I was frightened, who had never seen violence close up.

I went over to Vincenzo. Rapid, shallow breaths moved his chest. Two rivulets of blood dribbled from his nostrils to his open mouth, and one cheekbone was already swollen. His hand was still covered with sauce. I offered him the handkerchief I had in my pocket, but he turned the other way without accepting it. Then I sat on the floor, next to him, like a point near his silence. He knew I was there and didn't send me away.

"Next time I'll crush him," he promised himself, muttering, when he recognized the sound of his father getting up from the table. By now they had all finished. Adriana began to clear, while the baby, sleepy, started whining.

"If you don't eat that's your affair," the mother said passing by me, "but you wash the dishes just the same, today's your turn," and she pointed to the full sink. She and her son didn't even look at each other.

Vincenzo got to his feet and washed his face in the bathroom. With some pieces of rolled-up toilet paper he stopped up his nostrils and hurried to work, the lunch hour had been over for a while.

While Adriana rinsed the soapy plates that I handed her, she told me about our brother's escapes. The first time, at fourteen, he had followed the ride operators to a festival in the next town. He had helped them dismantle the amusement park and at the moment of departure had hidden in the back of a truck. He had emerged at the next stop, afraid of being sent home. But the Gypsies had kept him for a few days, and he worked with them, wandering through the county. When they put him on a bus home to his family, they had left him a precious object as a souvenir.

"Papa beat him," Adriana said, "but he kept the silver ring

with curious engravings. His friend you saw yesterday evening gave it to him."

"But Vincenzo doesn't wear a ring, it seems to me."

"He keeps it hidden. Sometimes he puts it on, then he rolls it between his fingers and hides it again."

"Where? You don't know?"

"No, he changes the place. It must be a magic ring, after he touches it he's happy for a while."

"Last night, too, he slept with the Gypsies?"

"I think so. Whenever he comes back with that pleased expression he's been with them. And yet he knows he'll get a beating."

The mother called her to collect the clothes hanging on the balcony. The tasks she asked me to do weren't many in comparison to Adriana's. Maybe she was sparing me, or maybe she forgot I was there. Certainly she didn't consider me capable, and she wasn't wrong. Sometimes I couldn't even understand her orders, in that rapid and contracted dialect.

"Do you remember the first time Vincenzo ran away from home?" I asked when Adriana came to the kitchen to put away the folded towels. "Was she in despair? Did they call the carabinieri?"

She scowled, and her eyebrows almost met in the center.

"No, the carabinieri no. Papa went looking for him in the car. She didn't cry, but she was silent," she answered, indicating with her chin the direction of the shouting in the other room.

In order to get at least a little sleep, I would remember the sea: the sea a few dozen meters from the house I'd thought was my home and had lived in since I was an infant until a few days earlier. Only the road separated the yard from the beach, and on days of *libeccio*, the southwest wind, my mother closed the windows and lowered the shutters completely to keep the sand from getting in. But you heard the sound of the waves, slightly muffled, and at night it made you sleepy. I remembered it in the bed with Adriana.

As if retelling fairy tales, I told her about walks along the sea with my parents to the most famous ice-cream shop in the city. She, in a dress with narrow shoulder straps, red nail polish on her toes, walking on his arm, while I ran ahead to get in line. Mixed fruit for me with whipped cream on top, French vanilla for them. Adriana couldn't imagine that all those flavors existed, I had to repeat them for her again and again.

"But where is that city?" she asked anxiously, as if it were a magical place.

"Fifty kilometers from here, more or less."

"You'll take me there sometime, so I'll get to see the sea, too. And the ice-cream shop."

I told her about dinners in the garden. I would set the table, while the bathers leaving the beach passed along the sidewalk a short distance away, beyond the gate. They shuffled their wooden clogs, shaking grains of sand from their ankles.

"And what did you eat?" Adriana wanted to know.

"Usually fish."

"Like canned tuna?"

"No, no, there's lots of others. We bought it fresh at the fish market."

I described cuttlefish, imitating the tentacles with my fingers. The contortions of mantis shrimp dying on the counters, as I watched them, spellbound. They stared at me, too, the two dark spots on the tail like reproachful eyes. On the way home, as my mother and I walked along the ballast of the railroad tracks, the bag rustled with their final spasms.

In describing it I thought I could taste in my mouth the flavor of the *frittura* that she prepared, and the stuffed calamari, the fish soups. Who knew how my mother was. Whether she'd started eating again, whether she was getting out of bed more often. Or if instead she'd been taken to the hospital. She hadn't wanted to tell me anything about her illness, certainly she didn't want to frighten me, but I had seen her suffering in the past months, she hadn't even gone to the beach, she who was usually there in the first warm days of May. With her permission I went to our umbrella by myself, since I was grown up now, she said. I had gone the day before my departure and had even had fun with my friends: I didn't believe that my parents would really find the courage to give me back.

I still had a tan, broken by the white skin in the shape of my bathing suit. That year I'd needed a bra, I was no longer a child. My brothers were dark, too, but only in the parts exposed during work or play outside. Their skin must have peeled at the start of the summer and then darkened again. Vincenzo had a permanent map of the sun's bites engraved on his back.

"Did you have friends in the city?" Adriana asked. She had just waved from the window at a schoolmate who was calling her from the big square.

"Yes, I did. Especially Patrizia."

In fact with her I'd picked out a two-piece bathing suit that spring. We'd gone to a store near the pool where we both swam. She was almost a champion, I went somewhat unwillingly. I was always cold: before I got into the pool, when I got out. I didn't like the gray inside, or the smell of chlorine. But I was homesick even for that, now that everything had changed.

Pat and I wanted to get matching bathing suits, to show up on the beach with our new shapes. We'd gotten our periods a week apart, and even the eruption of pimples seemed synchronized. Our bodies grew by mutual suggestion.

"This one is better for you," my mother had said, pulling out from among the other suits on the store's shelves a bikini that would give me more covering. "Because the skin on your breast is delicate, and in that one you'd burn." I remember every detail of that afternoon: the next day she got sick.

So I had given up the tiny two-piece, with bows between the cups and on the sides. Not Patrizia—she wanted it anyway. She often came to my house, I went less often to hers: my parents were afraid that her family's bad habits would rub off on me. They were cheerful, a little absentminded, disorderly. We never saw them at Mass on Sunday, not even at Easter or Christmas—maybe they didn't wake up in time. They ate what they felt like when they were hungry, they pampered two dogs and a rude cat that got up on the table to steal the leftovers. I remember the snacks we made by ourselves in the kitchen, spreading waves of chocolate on bread, even though it made our teeth hurt.

"This is what gives me energy for swimming," said Pat. "Take another piece, your mother won't know."

Only once did I have permission to stay overnight. Her parents had gone to the movies and we watched television until late, eating potato chips, then we stayed up talking from bed to bed for most of the night, the cat stretched out and purring on the blanket. I wasn't used to certain kinds of freedom, and at home the next day I nearly fell asleep over the chicken breast.

"Maybe those people gave you something?" my mother worried.

Patrizia thought it was a joke when I told her I had to go away. At first she didn't understand the story of a real family that was reclaiming me, and I understood less than she did, even when I heard the story told in my own voice just as I had learned it. I had to explain from the beginning, and Pat suddenly began sobbing, sobs that shook her whole body. Then I was really scared: I understood from her reaction that something serious was about to happen to me: she never cried.

"Don't be scared, your parents, I mean the ones here, won't allow it. Your father's a carabiniere, he'll find a way," she tried to console me after she recovered herself.

"He keeps saying he can't stop it."

"Your mother will be devastated."

"She hasn't been well for a while, maybe since she found out she can't keep me. Or maybe she decided to send me away because she's sick, and doesn't want me to know about it. I can't believe I have a family I've never seen and now suddenly they want me back."

"If I look at you, though, you don't look like either of your parents. Not the ones we know."

The idea came to me at night, I reported it to Patrizia in the morning under her umbrella. We perfected it in the smallest details, we were excited about our plan. After lunch I hurried to her house, without even asking permission from my mother, who was in her room resting. In those days she would have let me go anyway, with a weary yes, preoccupied with other things.

Pat opened the door with her head down, leaning against the frame. With a rude foot she pushed away the cat who was swishing his tail around her legs. I no longer wanted to go in. She took me by the hand and led me to the no that her mother was bound to give me. We girls had thought that the next day we'd return from the beach together, and I would stay hidden as long as necessary, even a month or two. If I disappeared, maybe all those parents would try harder to find a solution for me. I would even call my house—just once, though, and for a few seconds, as in a film—to reassure them and dictate my conditions.

"I won't go there. Either I come home to you or I'm going to run off into the world."

Pat's mamma hugged me tight, with her usual affection and a new embarrassment. She cleared off the couch and sat me down next to her. She even pushed away the cat: it wasn't his moment.

"I'm really sorry," she said. "You know how much I care about you. But it's impossible."

9.

"You weren't happy in the city?" Vincenzo asked me point-blank.

We were in the building's basement garage. In a shapeless heap against the walls were broken baskets, cartons corrugated by the dampness, a mattress full of holes with tufts of wool sticking out. A headless doll in a corner. In the small central area we kids were peeling tomatoes for sauce and cutting them up into pieces. I was the slowest.

"The little lady's never done it before," one brother had already mocked me, in a falsetto voice.

The baby stuck an arm in the bucket of peels and brought it to his mouth. The mother wasn't there just then: she'd gone to get something.

"So? Why'd you come back here?" Vincenzo persisted, pointing around with a red gesture.

"It wasn't my decision. My mother said I was grown up and my real parents wanted me back."

Adriana listened attentively with her eyes on me: she didn't have to look at her hands or at the knife she was using.

"Yeah, really! Get that out of your head, no one here ever dreamed of you," said Sergio, the cruelest. "Hey, Ma," he yelled outside, "for real you took back this moron?"

Vincenzo gave him a shove with his arm, and the other, laughing scornfully, fell off the overturned wooden crate he was sitting on. With one foot he knocked over a half-full container and some of the peeled tomatoes ended up on the concrete floor, in the dust. Without thinking, I was about to throw them in with the garbage, but Adriana took them away from me just in time, with a quick, adult move. She washed them and squeezed them before putting them back in the pot. She turned to stare at me in silence, had I understood? One mustn't waste anything. I nodded.

The mother returned with clean jars to fill. She had already stuck a basil leaf in each one.

"Oh goodness, have you got your period today?" she asked me curtly.

Embarrassed, I answered too softly.

"Well? Do you or not?"

I repeated no with my finger.

"That's lucky, otherwise it'll all be spoiled. Certain jobs you can't do if you have your period."

The jars of sauce sitting in water in a big pot over a fire in the corner between the building and the dirt embankment had just stopped boiling. Vincenzo appeared with half a bag of corn. He was looking back over his shoulder, and pretended not to hear anyone who asked where he'd gotten it. We cleaned off the beards and the husks; inside, the kernels were tender and sprayed milk if you tested them with a fingernail. I watched the others and imitated them. The edge of a leaf cut my skin, which was still soft.

Vincenzo roasted the corn on the remaining coals, occasionally turning them with his bare hands, a quick touch of his callused fingertips.

"If they get a little charred they're better," he explained to me, with a sidelong smile.

He waved the first one in front of Sergio's face; Sergio thought it was his, but it came to me. I burned myself.

"Serves you right," Sergio muttered waiting his turn.

"I've only had them once, but boiled. They taste much better this way," I said.

No one heard me. In silence I helped Adriana wash all the containers we'd used for the sauce and put them back in the garage.

"Forget Sergio, he's mean to everyone."

"Maybe he's right, maybe it wasn't your parents who asked to have me back. Now I'm sure of it, I'm here because my mother is sick. But I bet she'll come and get me when she's better."

D*ear Mamma or dear Aunt,*
I don't know what to call you anymore, but I want to come back to you. I don't like it in the town, and it's not true that your cousins expected me—in fact they see me as an annoyance, a nuisance for everyone, as well as one more mouth to feed.

You always said that for a girl the most important thing is personal cleanliness, so I'm letting you know that in this house it's even hard to wash. Two of us share a bed with a mattress that stinks of pee. The boys, who are fifteen and older, sleep in the same room, and you wouldn't like that. I don't know what might happen here. You who go to Mass every Sunday and teach catechism in the parish—you can't leave me in these conditions.

You're sick and you didn't want to tell me what's wrong, but I'm old enough to stay with you and help.

I understand that you took me when I was a baby for my own good, because I was born into a large, poor family. Here nothing has changed. If you care about me please send Uncle to get me, otherwise one of these days I'll jump out the window.

P.S. I'm sorry I wouldn't say goodbye to you the morning you made me leave, and thank you for the five thousand lire you put in with the handkerchiefs. What's left will be enough for the envelope and stamp.

I forgot to sign the letter, which was written on a sheet of paper torn from a lined notebook. I mailed it in the red box next to the door of the tobacco shop and counted the change, just the right amount for two popsicles, mint for me and lemon for Adriana.

"Who did you send it to?" she asked, carefully licking the paper she'd peeled off the frozen surface.

"To my mamma in the city."

"She's not a mamma."

"My aunt, then," I specified nervously.

"Yeah, she's a distant cousin of our father. Really the distant cousin is the husband, the one who brought you, the carabiniere. But she has the money, she's the one who takes care of you."

"What do you know about it?" The green liquid dripped along the stick, onto my fingers.

"Last night I heard a conversation in our parents' room. I was hiding in the closet because Sergio wanted to beat me up. It seems that this Adalgisa will also send you to the upper schools, poor you."

"What else did they say?" I asked, turning the popsicle upside down so that it wouldn't drip on my hand.

Adriana shook her head and took it away from me; she licked it all and gave it back, offering it to me with a gesture of impatience.

"With the trouble we're in, they kept saying."

I sucked what remained without wanting to, putting it all in my mouth for a while, until it was reduced to a ghost of colorless ice.

"Give it to me," Adriana said, exasperated, and finished it by taking little bites around the wooden stick.

I asked the mailman how long a letter would take to reach the city, doubled the number of days, and conceded one more for writing the answer. Then I began to wait for it, sitting on the wall every morning starting at eleven, while kids played tag or hopscotch in the big square. I swung my legs in the gentle

September sun and sometimes I imagined that, any moment, instead of a stamped envelope my uncle the carabiniere, who I'd thought was my father, would arrive. He would take me back in his long gray car and then I would forgive him for everything, for not having opposed my return, for leaving me there on the blacktop.

Or they would both come, she all better, her hair teased by the regular hairdresser, who also cut mine—my bangs had grown down over my eyes—and one of the soft scarves she wore between the seasons wrapped around her neck.

"What are you waiting for, a love letter?" the mailman joked after searching his leather bag in vain and disappointing me.

The delivery truck stopped under the blue sky, in the middle of the afternoon. The driver got out to ask what floor the recipient of the delivery lived on, the name was the mother's. He began to unload some cartons, while the kids immediately broke off their games to help him carry them up the stairs. We were all curious, and he enjoyed keeping us in suspense.

"Watch it, careful of the corners. Now when I put it together you'll see what it is," he repeated to the impatient among us.

"Where do the girls sleep?" he asked, as if following directions learned by heart.

Adriana and I opened the door to the room while looking at each other in disbelief. In a few minutes a bunk bed took shape before our eyes, complete with ladder and new mattresses. The man put it against the wall and arranged a folding screen with three panels around the free sides to separate it from the rest of the room. He went down to get something else; the answer to the letter was not yet complete.

"But who ordered all this stuff? And now who will pay for it?" Adriana was worried, as if waking suddenly from a dream. "Papa already has debts. And where did Mamma go?"

She had disappeared after lunch without a word, the baby in her arms. Maybe she was caught up in conversation at some neighbor's.

"Our parents didn't leave us the money," my sister began to explain to the man, who had carried up some more cartons, with the help of the same swarm of kids. They contained two sets of colored sheets, a wool quilt, a lighter blanket. This all seemed meant for only one of the bunk beds. There were also bars of soap, bottles of my favorite shampoo and anti-lice shampoo—I might need it here. And a sample of my mother's perfume: she knew that I used to steal a few drops in the morning before going to school.

"The items are already paid for. All I need is the signature of an adult to confirm the delivery."

Adriana took care of it, imitating the father's shaky writing. When we were alone in the room she asked to sleep on top, then on the bottom, then again on top. She had taken off her shoes and was trying out the positions, bustling up and down the ladder. We carried the old shapeless wire frame and the stinking mattress to the landing.

"I'm afraid I'll get the new one wet."

"She also bought a rubber sheet. You use it."

"Who bought—"

The mother returned at that moment, the sleeping baby's head dangling over her shoulder. She wasn't surprised by the new thing that Adriana wanted to show her immediately, tugging at her shirt. Irritated by her daughter's enthusiasm, she looked at the bed and the rest, and then at me, with a sort of dim condescension.

"That finicky aunt of yours sent it to you. Who knows what you told her about us. I talked to her yesterday on the public telephone, Signora Adalgisa had Ernesto in the wine shop call me."

The privilege of sleeping on mattresses fresh from the factory, enclosed by the screen, backfired on Adriana and me the first night. The boys hid behind that "thingy," as they called it, and frightened us by jumping out suddenly with a shout. They overturned it again and again, and within a week the fabric stretched between the sides of the panels was torn everywhere. They stuck their heads in the holes and yelled rudely. My sister and I witnessed the ruin of our small separate world: protests were useless to save it, and our parents didn't intervene. Years as an only child hadn't taught me to defend myself, and I endured the attacks, impotent and angry. When Sergio passed me, I was surprised that he wasn't struck down by my silent curses.

Only Vincenzo refrained from insults, and sometimes he shouted at his brothers to stop it, annoyed by their ruckus. After we carried the now useless screen down to the garage he looked at me for a long time, at night and when we woke up, as if he had missed the sight of my body. We still weren't wearing many clothes, because of the stubborn heat of that weary summer.

The bed so excited Adriana that she couldn't get to sleep on either the top or the bottom, and we were constantly changing places. At various times during the night she would come and curl up next to me, wherever I was. There was only one rubber sheet, so in a short time Adriana's involuntary urination soaked both new mattresses.

11

My seaside mother died on the upper bunk, on one of these nights. If you looked at her she didn't seem sick, maybe just a little grayer than usual. The hairy mole that extended over her chin like the incarnation of a caterpillar began to fade, slowly. In a few minutes it had turned pale, until it merged with the dark white around it. Air stopped inflating her chest and her gaze was fixed.

The other mother went with me to the funeral. *Pooradalgisa pooradalgisa*, she repeated, wringing her hands. But then she was expelled: she was wearing nylon stockings full of runs, and she couldn't be present at the service in that state. I remained alone, only daughter of the deceased. An indistinct group of black figures behind me took part in the ceremony. The gravediggers lowered the coffin into the newly dug hole, the ropes creaking under the weight, rubbing against the corners. I must have gotten too close to the edge of the grave: the grass gave way beneath me and I fell in, on top of her in that wooden box. I lay still, dazed and invisible. The priest gave a monotonous blessing and sprinkled holy water on my body, too. Then came the sound of the shovels, deaf to my cries, as they began to return the earth that had been moved. Finally someone grabbed me forcefully by one arm.

"If you don't stop screaming like a lunatic I'll throw you out the window," Sergio threatened, shaking me in the dark.

I didn't go back to sleep again. I followed the cold journey of the moon until it was hidden behind the wall.

The nightmare was the culmination of the anguish of my nights. After brief periods of giving into sleep, I would awaken with a jolt, convinced that some disaster was imminent, but what? I groped in those gaps of memory until my mother's illness returned suddenly to the surface and in the darkness intensified, worsened. During the day I could control it, believe in a cure, a return home afterward. At night she got sicker until she died in a dream.

Later I went down to Adriana, for once. She didn't wake up, she moved her feet to welcome me into our usual position, but I wanted to rest my head next to hers, on the pillow. I hugged her, to comfort myself. She was so small and bony, she smelled of greasy hair.

By contrast, Lidia's curls emerged from memory like red flowers between the sheets. She was the younger sister of my carabiniere father, but too young to be called aunt. For several years she had lived with us in my parents' house, and she appeared in my earliest memories. She had a long, narrow room at the end of the hall, with a view of the waves. In the afternoon I'd hurry to finish my homework and then we'd listen to songs on the radio. She was tormented, thinking of someone she'd lost, and she repeated the choruses of love sadly, with her fist on her asthmatic chest. Her parents had sent her away from their town to her brother's, to breathe the salt air.

When we were alone Lidia would put on a miniskirt and platform sandals that she kept hidden in the closet and turn the record player up loud. She did the Shake in the dining room, jerking up and down with her eyes closed. Who knows where she'd learned it—she wasn't allowed to go out after sunset, but sometimes she disobeyed, jumping out a ground-floor window. I wanted her next to me every night: just when I was about to fall asleep I got itches at inaccessible points on my back. Lidia came to scratch me and then she'd stay, sitting on the bed. She counted my vertebrae, I was so thin, and for each one she made up a story. She called the most prominent by name and had them converse like old ladies, touching one and then another.

"They'll take me," she said one day, coming home.

That's how I lost her, to a department store, a few years before I was returned. We had gone shopping early one morning, and while I was trying on a T-shirt with a fish-and-starfish pattern, she had asked a clerk if she could talk to the manager. The manager would be in later, and we waited for her. As soon as she received us in her unadorned office, Lidia took a secretarial diploma out of her purse and asked for a job, any sort of job. She sat across the desk and I stood next to her, and every so often she caressed my arm.

They called her almost immediately for a brief trial. One evening she came home with the uniform quivering in her hands; she would wear it the next day. She tried it on, walking back and forth in the living room. It was blue and white, with starched collar and cuffs. Now, like her brother, she, too, had a uniform. She performed a series of pirouettes to show off the flared skirt, and continued pirouetting through life for years after that. But, of course, I wasn't there to see any of it.

She advanced quickly from clerk to cashier and after a year was made head of the department. She came home later and later. Then she was transferred to the head office, several hundred kilometers away. She wrote to me sometimes, and I didn't know what to answer. At school everything's fine, yes. Patrizia's my friend as always, of course. In the pool I had learned to do somersaults, but I was still cold. At first she sent postcards of the monuments of the city, then they must have run out. In my notebooks I colored the sun as black as my mood, and the teacher telephoned the house to ask if someone had died. I had an average of ten, the highest mark, on my report card; I filled the time emptied by Lidia with painstaking attention to my assignments.

She returned in August for the holidays, but I was afraid to be happy with her again. We went to our regular beach and she got sunburned in spite of the creams she had bought with her employee discount. To the usual attendants who greeted her she spoke with the false northern accent of émigrés. I was ashamed for her and began to kill my nostalgia.

I saw her only one other time before they decided to give me back. She rang the bell and I opened the door to an unknown woman with dyed and straightened hair. Clinging to her legs was a little girl who wasn't me.

In the dark with Adriana, I imagined that Lidia would be able to rescue me, maybe take me to live with her for a while, in the north. But she had moved to another city and I no longer knew how to track her down. It was still too soon to imagine a different deliverance.

12

They turned off the light and jumped into bed. Sergio silenced his brother as I came into the room, but laughter escaped, muffled by the pillows. Vincenzo had been out since the afternoon and Adriana was still in the other room, with the baby. I undressed in the dark and in that charged silence got between the sheets. My foot touched something warm and furry, alive, which moved and whirred. I heard myself scream and the two boys sneering scornfully, and at the same time felt little pecks on my ankle. I don't know how I got to the light switch and turned to look at the bed. A pigeon was spinning around, hopping, flapping one wing, spread as if it would be enough to fly. The other hung next to the body, broken. Excrement was on the new sheet. The bird reached the edge of the mattress and fell off, landing on its chest.

The brothers were sitting up, howling with rude laughter; they slapped their thighs and tears rolled down their faces. The animal kept it up, on the floor, trying to lift off. Tired of the spectacle, Sergio picked it up by the healthy wing and threw it out the window. At that moment I was sure that he had broken the other one.

I got too close to him, yelling that he was a monster and scratching his face with all my nails, leaving furrows in his skin that immediately began to bleed. He didn't defend himself, he didn't hit me; he laughed again, exaggerating a little to show that I couldn't hurt him. The other one jumped on the beds like a monkey, imitating the sound of a pigeon.

The father came to see. Even before finding out what had happened he hit them both, just to settle them. By a silent agreement, ever since the boys were grown and his wife was no longer strong enough, he had been the one to give the beatings. She took care of Adriana, with a more or less daily dose.

"It was just a little joke," Sergio explained, "at night she screams for no reason and wakes us up. So I scared her and made her scream."

The next day I helped fold the sheets that had already dried.

"Watch out for the bedbugs," the mother said, chasing away a pretty green one. "I don't know why they like to get in the middle of the hanging laundry." She passed naturally from the bugs to her sons. "That second one came out all wrong. The other one every so often runs away, but he's not too bad."

"They don't want me here, in this house, that's why they torture me. Why don't you send me back where I was?"

"Eventually even Sergio will get used to it. But try not to cry out in your sleep, it gets on his nerves."

She stopped for a moment, with the pile of laundry in her arms. She looked me in the eyes—which she rarely did—as if following a thought.

"Do you remember when we met at the wedding? You might have been six, seven."

She reopened my memory with a lash of the whip.

"I remember something, only here you're different, in your everyday clothes. That time you looked elegant," I admitted.

"I can't tell you how many times I wore that suit. At a certain point I put on some weight and I was afraid the seams would burst." She smiled. "It was a Sunday in June, the bride and bridegroom had wasted time with all that picture-taking," she began to recount. "Everyone had gotten so hungry, at three we were still looking for seats in the restaurant. All of a sudden

I turn around and see you, I didn't recognize you, you'd gotten so big and pretty."

"How did you know it was me?"

"First of all I had a feeling, and then there was Adalgisa, you know? She was talking to a relative and didn't notice me right away. I called you, and you looked up. You were surprised, maybe because there were tears in my eyes."

Today I would ask for every last detail of that encounter, but at the time I was too confused. She continued on her own, she had put the laundry down on a chair.

"As soon as she saw me, Adalgisa got in the middle, between you and me. But you peeked out from behind her with that curious little head and looked at me."

I stared obliquely at a lock of hair on her forehead, white before its time, as a sign of recognition all its own. When I was returned to her it was beginning to blend in with her hair, which was prematurely gray, and would soon be lost in its total whiteness.

That day at the wedding I didn't know anything. My fathers were distant cousins; I bore their surname. During the month when I was weaned the two families divided up my life with a few promises: without specifying anything, and without wondering what I would pay for their vagueness.

"I couldn't say too much, because you were small, but I gave your aunt a piece of my mind."

"Why?"

"She had sworn that you would always come here to us, that we'd bring you up together. But the only time we saw you was at your first birthday. We went to the city." Her voice failed, for a few seconds. "But afterward you moved and no one let us know."

I listened carefully, intent on her story, but I didn't want to trust her. Adriana had said so, the day I arrived, not to believe too much of what she said.

"She used the excuse that she had a sick sister-in-law and couldn't leave her, but, just as she said it, Lidia came over to greet me, so pretty, and in good health."

"Lidia had asthma, sometimes they had to take her to the emergency room," I replied curtly.

She looked at me and added nothing else. She understood which side I was on. She picked up the pile of laundry from the chair and carried it into her room.

13.

After my letter with no response, there must have been some new arrangements that I didn't know about. Every Saturday the mother in the town was obliged to give me a small sum, which came by some means or other from the mother on the coast. Clutching it in my hands, sometimes a little reduced by the one who delivered it, I felt reassured about the health of my distant mamma: maybe she was getting better. And I was always in her thoughts. I believed that I was receiving, along with the coins, the warmth of her palm, preserved in the metal of the hundred-lire pieces, as if she really had touched them.

I exchanged a nod of understanding with Adriana and we went to Ernesto's wine shop. I opened the ice cream refrigerator and searched through the cold white vapor. Two ice cream pops with a crunchy coating, chocolate for me, cherry for her: we ate them there, sitting at a table outside, like the old men absorbed in their card game. The rest I set aside, or sometimes I'd buy a pacifier for Giuseppe, who was always losing his.

In a few weeks I had scraped together enough money for bus tickets and some sandwiches. Adriana got scared when I told her, so we proposed to Vincenzo that he come with us. He was taking the last drags of a cigarette at the end of the big square, before coming up to dinner. He blew out the smoke with his eyes closed, as when he was reflecting.

"O.K., but no one at home has to know where we're going," he agreed, surprisingly. "We'll tell them you're coming to work in the countryside with me—they don't give a damn anyway," he added, with a dark look up at the second floor.

At dawn we got on the bus for the city. Adriana had never seen the city, Vincenzo only certain outlying neighborhoods where his Gypsy friends camped with the rides. The bus stop was very close to the beach club where I had spent all my summers. From our lotion-perfumed shade my mother and I watched the swarms of bathers marching toward the stretch of free beach beyond the roped enclosure. On those end-of-season days we'd eat grapes, picking them one at a time from the bunches she'd brought.

There was no one there, so early. A new girl was sweeping the concrete walkway between the sidewalk and the entrance to the café. The attendant was opening the umbrellas with their green and yellow sections, one metallic click after another. He didn't open mine, in the first row, as if he knew there was no point.

"Hey, here you are, where'd you go?" when I went by. "You all really disappeared, not even your mother's been here—were you on vacation somewhere? Anyway, I'll open it right away, number seven."

The lounge chair squeaked from disuse. Suddenly the man in the faded shirt turned to the two who were following me, several steps behind: they were different from the usual clientele.

"They're my cousins, they live in the mountains," I said softly.

Captivated by the novelties, they wouldn't have heard it anyway. They sat on the sand, even Vincenzo slightly intimidated. Small lazy waves licked the shore, without foam and without sound. The sun was still low above the horizon, and seagulls perched on the rocks of the breakwater.

"If the water comes over will we die?" Adriana asked, frightened. She let the fine sand run between her fingers, in disbelief. We took off our clothes: she had on a bathing suit that no longer fit me, and Vincenzo wore his underpants. We hung the clothes on the ribs of the umbrella; a hair band I thought I'd lost was knotted around the pole. Here it was. I struggled to loosen it with my bitten nails; I put it in my purse. I'd had it for years. When I was younger my mother would comb my hair and then put on the hair band, grazing my face with her hands. Every morning she sat on the edge of my bed and I'd stand in front of her. The sound of the brush on my head was pleasant, with the faint vibration of the metal teeth.

My sister didn't want to go swimming or even get her feet wet, afraid that the sea would suck her in. She crouched on the dry sand, chin on her knees, her gaze dissolved in all that blue. Silently I went in, gliding under the water for the length of a breath, without disturbing the surface. Then, with my head out, I saw the beach filling up with early risers, Adriana squatting, waiting for my return, Vincenzo's impetuous run and a dive that sent water spraying into the air. He had learned to swim at the river, with his friends. He headed toward me with powerful, uneven arm strokes, tracing a line in the sea. When he'd almost reached me he disappeared for a second, and, sticking his neck between my legs, suddenly lifted me up. I found myself on his shoulders, as he kept himself afloat, spitting water. We didn't feel the cold.

"It was great of you to bring us here," he said. "I'm really having a good time."

He slipped away and, showing off, did handstands and somersaults; he grabbed me by the waist and threw me like a toy, again and again. He laughed, and the salt whitened his gums. My foot accidentally touched him near his penis, it was swollen and bulging. He covered my ears with his hands and kissed me on the lips, then his tongue went into my mouth and explored it, circling it with desire. He had forgotten who we were.

I swam away, without hurry or disgust. Only on the shore did I realize that my heart was still beating rapidly. Adriana was sitting there, as I had left her. Maybe not much time had passed, even if the world seemed different. I lay down on the sand next to her, waiting for the confusion in my breast to settle.

"I'm hungry," she said, whining.

I had sandwiches in my bag, but to cheer her up I took her to the café and got a pizza and Coke, with the last of the money. When we returned to the umbrella, Vincenzo came out of the water, exhausted, like a rough, wild god who had descended to the sea for a single day. If now I remember his tired steps, I imagine that he left the blue expanse behind him fecund. A few people noticed him; his underpants clung too closely to the shape of his body and the waistband was lowered to reveal a strip of hair. But the sweaty crowd of August was no longer here, in this serene close of summer. Now clandestine on the beach that had brought me up, I could avoid being recognized by the regular swimmers. Vincenzo and I also avoided each other, for the rest of the day. I put out the sandwiches, without saying anything. I took Adriana to the swings and, making some excuse, left her.

I only had to cross and take the street almost opposite. I walked alongside the garden fence, looking at the signs of abandonment. A chair overturned by the wind, the table we would set when we were having dinner outside scattered with the first fallen leaves. A rag stuck on the thorns of the rose, my mother's favorite flower—in the month of May she'd pin a bud to her bosom before going out. The grass was tall and the flowers, unwatered, were dead and dry. I arrived at the gate with lead in my feet. The mailbox wasn't too full, maybe someone was picking up the letters now and then: mine, too, had been received. The path was invaded by sand the *libeccio* blew in, the shutters were all pulled down, as when we left for vacation.

Sheltered under the eaves was my bicycle, with one tire flat. I rang the bell into the emptiness of the rooms and after a vain wait rang it over and over again, for a long time. I leaned my forehead against the bell and stood like that until the heat became unbearable. I ran back across the street, nearly getting run over, and sat down in the shade of the cabanas.

She must be dead, then, as in my dream, like her tulips, otherwise she wouldn't have abandoned the house. But it was she who had sent me the bunk bed and everything else, and the other mother said that they had talked on the phone. Why didn't she talk to me, too? Where was she? Maybe she didn't want to upset me with a sick voice, from a distant hospital. Or what if, rather, my father had been transferred to another city? He said it was possible. No, they would have taken me with them wherever. And did Lidia know? Did she know and not look for me? But they didn't talk often. Shortly before she was transferred to the north she'd gotten up to one of her old tricks, and maybe my mother had never completely forgiven her.

Lidia had met Lili Rose, a dancer who lived in the attic apartment of the building across the street, and sometimes they talked furtively through the gate of our garden. Lili Rose worked in a nightclub on the beach and slept until afternoon. Every so often refined-looking men discreetly rang her bell. Lidia wasn't allowed even to say hello to her, for fear she'd be contaminated.

But one hot, muggy Sunday my parents went to a funeral and left us at home. Lili Rose came to ask if we'd also lost our running water—her taps were dry. Above her eyes, smudged by the makeup of the night before, was a tangle of bleached hair, and she was scantily dressed. Lidia had invited her in, offered her a cold drink and then a shower. Lili Rose came out of the bathroom barefoot and dripping, with my mother's bathrobe half open in front.

They started dancing in the living room, sedately at first,

then more closely entwined, to the slow, sensual rhythms of particular records. With her pelvis thrust forward Lili Rose showed how to move and rub against a man's body. She stuck her leg out through the opening in the terry cloth, and rubbed it against Lidia's, but in fun, for laughs. As the minutes passed, I felt a little nervous and kept looking at the door. Not them. They had pushed the coffee table to one side and moved on to a frenetic and pounding Shake, jerking as if possessed. Lidia had taken off her sweaty shirt, and was in short shorts and bra. At the end of a 45 they collapsed on top of each other on the sofa, panting. The belt of the bathrobe had come loose around Lili Rose's waist and exposed it.

My mother, returning early from the funeral, had found them like that.

I stayed behind the cabanas. Adriana, wandering around in tears, ran into me by chance. She must have fallen off the swing; she hadn't even wiped the sand off her lips and nose. In that alien setting she was defenseless, and hadn't been able to find the umbrella in the first row, where she could have waited for me with her brother.

"I didn't fall off by myself, those guys pushed me," she complained when we reached him. "They said this wasn't my beach and I couldn't go on the swing." She pointed to some boys who were hanging around the playground area.

He charged like a bull. I don't know if they exchanged some words or immediately started fighting. When Adriana and I got there they were rolling around on the ground, locked in struggle like statues of sand, many against one, ours. We called the owner of the beach club, he shouted at them and pulled them apart. But afterward, taking me aside, he told me not to bring that half Gypsy in underpants here again, who was he? Certainly not a relative of such a respectable family, and my father a carabiniere.

Vincenzo washed in the shallow water, without the pleasure of a swim. In the middle of the afternoon people under the neighboring umbrellas were eating melon, and they looked at us. The man with the whistle passed by, walking along the shore hawking fresh coconut.

"Is he selling fresh eggs?" Adriana was amazed.

"No, it's an exotic fruit." But I didn't have enough change.

He smiled at my sister's curiosity as she approached the bucket and gave her a piece, a small one, for her first taste.

We got dressed and set off toward the bus stop, and for a second I thought I heard behind us a general sigh of relief. From the window I waved at the five-story building where Patrizia lived and silently promised I would come back to see her.

"I'll take the later bus, I'm going to see some friends," Vincenzo said, standing up suddenly to get out at one of the stops on the outskirts. Seeing him on the sidewalk through the dusty glass, all bruised, I no longer knew what I felt. Looking at me, he touched his lips with an index finger while the driver started off, and I don't know if he wanted to blow me a kiss or tell me to be silent.

Adriana slept until we reached the town, but at night she complained because of the irritation of her sunburn. At home no one paid attention, the mother asked only if we had brought some fruit from the countryside. Vincenzo returned after two days and the father didn't punish him; maybe he hadn't noticed, or by now he had given up correcting that son.

14

C ome down, I have to show you something, behind the garage," he called from below the window.
  I went down a little later with Adriana and he gave me a dirty look.

He sent her to buy him some cigarettes in the square, she could keep the change. Vincenzo must have had a lot of money in his pocket: when he was reaching in for the coins a banknote fell out. With a glance he blocked my intention to follow Adriana.

"She's still too young, she doesn't know how to keep a secret," he said when she turned the corner. "Now wait here for me."

He returned quickly, with his habit of glancing back suspiciously, to one side and then the other. Taking a blue velvet bag from under his armpit, he knelt on the ground to open it and show me his treasure. He lined up the pieces on the strip of cement around the building, as if on the counter of a jewelry store. They must have been secondhand: their brilliance seemed slightly diminished. With delicate fingers he unknotted two tangled necklaces and laid them down next to each other. Finally, pleased, he admired his small display of bracelets, rings, and chains, some with pendants and some without, before turning to see the effect of this spectacle of gold on me. He was surprised to find me silent and anxious.

"What's wrong, you don't like it?" he asked, standing up in disappointment.

"Where'd you get it?"

"I didn't get it, I was paid, with these," he explained with the expression of an offended child.

"They're worth a lot of money. You can't earn that much in two days."

"My friends wanted to thank me before they left. I'd helped them, you know, for nothing."

"What are you going to do with the stuff now?" I persisted.

"Resell it," and he knelt again to pick up the jewelry.

"Are you nuts? If you get caught with stolen goods, you'll end up in the reformatory."

"Oo-ooh, what do you know about it? Who says it's stolen, anyway?" And he turned to show me two bracelets that he was holding in his trembling hand. His nostrils, too, were quivering above his new beard.

"You can tell. And then my father is a carabiniere, he's always talking about how the Gypsies rob houses." It escaped, just like that: I made a mistake again in naming my adoptive parents.

"Yeah, lucky you, still thinking about your father the carabiniere. That guy, your uncle, doesn't even remember you. He never comes to see how you're doing here."

Tears fell, catching me unawares—I hadn't felt them coming. Vincenzo had spoken like Sergio, but he immediately got up and came over. He dried my face, brushing his thumbs roughly over the skin, and repeating no, head and voice contrite, don't cry, he couldn't bear it. Wait, wait, he said, and he finished picking up his jewels and putting them back in the blue bag. All except one.

"I called you down to give you this, first, but you made me mad . . . " and he came over with a precious heart hanging on a chain.

I swerved instinctively, a step back and sideways, and he stood with the gold tie suspended in the air, the pendant dangling. His forehead was contracted into a crowd of stormy frowns, his mouth reduced to a slash. On his temple the fish bone pulsed, red with rekindled rage. But I also recognized in his eyes a painful, defenseless astonishment. I moved forward with an equal and opposite step, I lifted my chin to receive the gift. The contact of his oddly capable hands as they clasped the chain behind my neck without looking. On my chest moments of coolness in the shape of a heart, then the metal was warmed by the deep blood that moved it with small frequent regular pulses.

"It looks really lovely on you," Vincenzo said, in a low voice.

With slow fingers he drew on my skin the outline of the pendant, then wanted to go down toward my breasts.

"Here's your cigarettes," Adriana arrived, running.

She stopped suddenly; I don't know what she saw.

"The cigarettes," she repeated slowly, handing him the pack uncertainly.

She was still holding in her teeth the stick of the cherry popsicle she'd bought with the change. I turned my back to her and unclasped the gift from around my neck, hiding it in my pocket. I almost never put it on, and yet I still have it, a possibly stolen object. I don't know how I've managed to keep it for twenty years, taking it everywhere with me. I'm fond of it. I've used it as a talisman on some occasions, my final exams in high school, some important appointments. I'll wear it again at Adriana's wedding, if it's true that she wants to get married. I have no idea who this heart once belonged to.

I avoided being alone with Vincenzo, in those days, but whenever I saw him appear an internal spasm wrung my guts and immediately a kind of languor flooded my stomach. Toward evening he whistled to me through the windows on the garage side, and it took an effort of will to ignore him. After a short, vain wait he came in, silent, furious, slamming the door.

He gave off a current that caused the sudden fall of a pot from the hook on the wall, wailing for no reason from Giuseppe, an inexplicable headache in Adriana. I resisted, at a distance.

The Saturday money was enough for a bus ticket. I told the parents the truth, that I wanted to go to the birthday party of a friend from before. I asked if I could stay overnight. They looked at each other for moment, with that apathetic uncertainty.

"I can't take you, the car won't start" was the father's permission. From the strange sound of his voice I realized that he almost never spoke.

I went down early in the morning; from the window I'd seen something bright-colored to pick for Patrizia on the slope behind the building. I couldn't give her anything else. They were dandelions and some other small yellow flowers that smelled of turnips. I tied up the bouquet with string and went back upstairs to get ready. Adriana knew nothing about my plans, and when she realized where I was going without her she ran to the bedroom to get a drawing I had made for her and tore it up under my nose. To my surprise the mother wanted to come with me to the bus stop in the square, carrying the baby. I said goodbye from the window of the bus and he moved his hands in that repetitive way he had, which didn't seem like waving.

During the journey the flowers wilted and people in the nearby seats stared at them, maybe because of the smell. As I waited for the door to open on the fifth floor of the building on the northern shore, I no longer even knew whether to give them to her, to my friend.

She rushed at me and shouted with joy, the dogs barked in excitement and the cat came to see. Eyes lowered I apologized for the poverty of the gift, but, hopping up and down, she swore that the best of all her presents was me.

We spent the morning alone, talking nonstop, though I had slightly less to say. I was ashamed to tell her about my new life, and so I asked desperately about hers. I rediscovered the smells of the house, cinnamon in the kitchen, a slightly sour odor of sweat in Patrizia's room, and in the bathroom her mother's No. 5 perfume, which she always put on before she went to the office. I was a day late for the birthday party, but in the refrigerator were delicious leftovers, salty and sweet, that we nibbled on for hours, lying on the bed. Pat told me about the swimming competitions she'd won—I would have come in third or fourth if I'd entered. We laughed at the boy with the long nose who'd been coming on to her for months.

"How can he kiss me with that snout?" she wondered, uncertain whether to give him the chance.

"When you weren't there . . . ": so began the story of every episode, as if my absence were now an irreversible fact.

15.

The cat meowed, rubbing against his mistress, but it got a distracted caress and nothing to eat. We had forgotten all about the passing day, Pat was still in her pajamas. The sound of the door and then of the keys placed on the shelf in the front hall finally dislodged us from the world à deux we had already reconstructed. Vanda was moved and held me tight for a long time, infusing me with her French perfume. I closed my eyes, lost in the embrace of her white linen shirt as long as it lasted. She knew I wasn't bitter; I'd forgiven her refusal to hide me in her house without even a thought.

"Let me look at you," she said afterward, taking a step back.

She found me taller and only a little thinner. By chance she'd stopped at the rosticceria and bought eggplant parmigiana, one of my favorite dishes. She watched me, smiling, while I ate; she'd given up her share with the excuse of a diet that had already been put off too long. In the meantime Pat's father called: we wouldn't see him till evening. I ate his share, too, and cleaned the plate with a piece of bread. My friend was surprised—I didn't use to do that.

"In the town that's what they do," I explained, uneasily.

Vanda was gently curious about my natural family and I was less evasive with her. I lowered my guard slightly, then suddenly felt ashamed again. With that shame I began to acknowledge my first parents.

I said the names of the other children, telling them a little about Adriana and Giuseppe. I didn't know I was describing the two of them with pity and tenderness, especially her. My sister, I called her. About Vincenzo I said nothing.

"And your parents?" Finally we were there.

"I haven't heard from them, after my father brought me there."

"No, I meant the ones you're with now."

"He works at the brick factory, but not always, I think," and I broke off. I excused myself and went urgently to the bathroom, but only to close myself in and wait a little, sniffing the perfumed jars. I flushed the toilet and went back. As I'd expected, Vanda was now involved in something else.

Later Patrizia asked her to take us to the port to see the procession of boats: the local fishermen's festival was on. After Mass at the nearest church, the flagship, decked with flowers, set off with the statue of the saint and the priest, followed by the fleet of fishing boats, all of them, including the smallest, decorated with multicolored flags flying in the wind. Pat and I ran after them, along with the crowd on the pier, then we left them to continue north, skirting the beach. Before returning they would lower a laurel wreath into the water in memory of those lost at sea. The fishermen's wives were selling fried fresh fish: Patrizia bought a portion in a paper cone, and the tiny bones of the sprats tickled our tongues. At dinner we ate again, in order not to disappoint Vanda, who had made a gratin with fresh razor clams that her husband had brought.

"I saw your father last week," Nicola said. "He was at a blockade outside the city."

"Did you talk to him?" I asked anxiously.

"No, he was stopping a truck. He's let his beard grow."

"Don't think about it now," Pat shook me after a dirty look at her father. "Let's get ready, let's go back to the festival. You can wear something of mine."

We wouldn't miss the fireworks display at the end this year, either.

"The car will be useless," Nicola said, so I got on the handlebars of his bicycle and the two others followed. He pedaled almost effortlessly, ringing the bell to alert the pedestrians who were heading toward the port in increasing numbers. We advanced silently and smoothly, amid the lights and the sugary smells of the first stalls: cotton candy, almond brittle. Sometimes the gaseous overflow of a sewer. Then we couldn't advance any farther along the wide sidewalk by the shore, and we got off the bikes and chained them to the bars of a beach club. Patrizia and I wanted to go off on our own, so her parents set a time for us to meet them after the fireworks. We waited for the start sitting on the beach in an imaginary first row, as the crowd slowly gathered behind us, expectant. On both sides of us were other kids; a boy with glasses and curly hair who looked like a high-school student leaned forward every so often to look at me sideways.

"That curly-haired guy likes you," Pat laughed, winking in his direction.

I encircled her shoulders and hugged her hard, for a moment. I couldn't tell her what I missed, her and the life I'd been sent away from. Maybe she saw the tears that I tried to hide.

"What's wrong?" she asked, and I didn't answer.

Some preparations announced the show, and a wave of excitement passed through the crowd. We stood up, eyes on the darkness over the sea. The fireworks began quietly, as if at a rehearsal, going off in bursts, and then steadily reaching a crescendo. After a moment of glory, universes of exploded stars faded against the cold background of fixed celestial bodies. Underwater, far from our thoughts, the mute fear of the fish.

Suddenly a live, decisive hand clasped mine, and I turned smiling to Pat, whom I hadn't seen for a few minutes. It wasn't her: it was the boy with the curly hair, fireworks reflected in the lenses of his glasses. In my memory I can feel again the spasm in my stomach, slightly diminished at the distance of years. He had chosen me, among all those girls.

"What's your name?" he said in my ear, with his voice and the sweet breath from his mouth. His delicate features changed color from moment to moment, like the marvels in the sky.

Who knows if he heard the answer in the din of the last round of explosions. I couldn't read his in the movement of his lips, Mario, maybe, or Massimo. From the hand that he held tight for a few moments a hot shiver traveled through my arm to my heart. Someone bumped into him and the kiss directed at my face was lost in the air. We immediately lost each other, too, in the final crush that cleared the beach. I had to look for Patrizia, and he wasn't able to stay beside me. He might have been the same age as Vincenzo: he was so different.

I hadn't slept the long deep sleep of that night since I'd been returned. With the light of dawn the subtle anguish of another day filtered through the blinds, slipped under the covers of the guest bed. I woke up dazed, as if I'd been drunk. In the afternoon I had to go back to the town. I sat at the breakfast table with Vanda, the only one who was already up.

"You haven't seen my mother in all this time?"

"Never, not since you were with her," and she served me warm milk and cocoa.

"Have you ever passed by my street?"

"Yes, but the house was always shuttered." She gave me bread and jam, biscuits in the shape of a flower.

"Maybe they're treating her in a hospital far away and my father went with her."

"Why do you think that?"

"They didn't ask for me back, in the town, and she had no reason to give me back. Maybe she hid the truth so as not to scare me, but in the last weeks she didn't have the energy for cooking or cleaning. She was in bed and was crying for me." I stopped to rub my eye. "But I'm sure that when she's better they'll come and get me and reopen the house," I concluded.

Vanda drank her coffee thoughtfully. A small brown stain remained on her nose.

"In time it will all be clearer," she said. "Now try to hold out, at least for the school year that's starting. Then, with your grades, you'll have to come to high school in the city, one way or another."

I nodded, with my head over the milk that was getting cold, and barely a drop in my mouth.

"Now eat. You'll see they'll let you come back to us again."

Later I asked Patrizia if she wanted to go to my house, which wasn't far. She was excited, as if we were off on a daring mission.

"Shall I bring a screwdriver?" she asked in the low voice of a secret agent; in her view we'd have to force the lock on the gate.

But it was already open, and there were sounds coming from the back. We went in cautiously, Pat imitating the manner of a spy in a film. We walked along the path. The sand had been swept up, the garden tidied, the low grass smelled of recent cutting. A rake was leaning against the wall, with other tools. The house was closed, though, the shutters lowered. Under the eaves my bicycle had been moved slightly, the tire had been filled, the pump was on the ground nearby. Sound of repeated blows from the back, then nothing. Again. Holding my breath, my mouth dry, I was about to meet my father. He often hammered like that, making small household repairs.

At the corner of the house wall a collision, a shout, and I found myself in the arms of Romeo, the gardener. Patrizia instead lost her balance and was sitting on the lawn, looking at us.

"Hey, pretty miss, where'd you come from? It didn't seem anyone was home. Can you call your mother? I'm done here."

"My parents aren't home right now," I improvised. "Who gave you the key?"

"Your father left it in a café. He telephoned to ask me to clean up the garden before the fall."

"Do you have the door key?"

"No, not that one," and he must have become suspicious. "But are you here alone?" and he pointed to the house.

"No, I'm staying with my friend, we came to get some books. Anyway you can leave the key with me, Papa and Mamma will be back tomorrow." I thought I was lying with some naturalness, but he didn't fall for it.

"Better if I take it back to the same café, the way I agreed with the marshal."

So he removed the possibility of going into the garden, at least. I didn't correct him on my father's rank.

At lunch I struggled to twist the spaghetti with clams around my fork. Nicola knew how much I liked it and begged me to eat. A listless anxiety made a lump in my throat. On the TV there was talk about new anti-terrorism laws, then a report on the first big new amusement park in Italy, which had recently opened.

"We can't miss it," Pat said. "They organize one-day bus trips—we'll go one of the next times you come."

And we did go, but many years later. I had just finished a round of exams at the university, I came from Rome and we went together. The lake was an unusual destination for two girls, but Patrizia had been wounded in love and found the landscape of still water fitting for her mood.

"Enough of this morgue, today let's go to Gardaland," she decided one morning on the terrace of our little hotel, with geraniums in the windows. At the entrance we mingled with children. I screamed with fear even on the most predictable of rides, the roller coaster, where, at the highest point on the panoramic track, you were still for a few seconds, hovering in space. But nothing brought back the emotion of that night with Vincenzo and Adriana, on the Gypsies' jangling chair swing.

I got the bus at one of the stops along the sea. They all three insisted on coming with me; Vanda even brought the dogs on leashes. I had arrived with some flowers from the hillside, I returned to the town with a supply of notebooks, underwear, shirts and pants, and a bag to hold them, which would also be useful for school. As we said goodbye a sob escaped me: I couldn't muffle it. I would have preferred to drown in the blue that was thirty meters of sand from the sidewalk.

I see myself again, sitting in a window seat, my head leaning against the glass. Nicola had given me a package of cookies and, from the regular rosticceria, a generous helping of egg-plant parmigiana. I decided to give it to my sister, in an attempt to mollify her. Maybe that evening we could eat it secretly, she and I, down in the garage. I would give her some notebooks and lend her the bag. The idea of seeing her again, armed with her jealousy, frightened me. Adriana was all I had, at the end of the bus ride. Meanwhile I could cry without embarrassment along the twisting road; the seat next to me remained empty.

16

S he had gone up to the square to wait for the arrival of every bus coming from the city, starting in the late morning. I didn't see her at first in the half light of the September sunset; she was standing a short distance away. I was already starting toward home when she took a step and I noticed her, fists clenched at the ground, eyes invisible under frowning eyebrows. We stood looking at each other, a few meters apart, and I didn't know whether to approach that lump of bitter rage and weariness. I felt that she was observing with her voracious rapidity the bursting bag, the packages I had trouble carrying. Then unexpectedly she ran up and hugged me. I put everything down on the asphalt, hugged her tight and kissed her forehead. We went on side by side, without saying anything; she helped me with the bag and the rest of the packages, but she didn't want to know right away what they contained. She spoke only when we reached the big square, inspecting them with a sweeping glance. But no one was there at that hour, they were having dinner.

"Better hide that stuff downstairs, otherwise it'll meet a bad end," and she pointed to the second floor, thinking of Sergio and the other.

We opened the garage with the key that was always left behind a brick and got rid of everything.

"Don't eat too much," I said on the stairs. "I have something good for you, later."

Upstairs, the family didn't seem to have suffered from my

absence. Only Giuseppe pulled away from his mother's breast, losing his balance as he leaned toward me. I picked him up and he stuck a sticky, sweetish hand in my mouth.

"The little lady ate fish," Sergio pronounced quickly when I wasn't hungry at supper. "Raw fish," he added, in order not to leave doubts.

Vincenzo wasn't there. After dinner and our tasks, Adriana and I went downstairs with an excuse that wasn't needed. She had hidden some forks in her clothes; and, sitting on an overturned basket, she tasted her first eggplant parmigiana: she ate all of it, understanding that I was giving up my share. The burp that escaped her afterward sounded like forgiveness for my two days of absence.

The next morning we had to take care of the baby: the mother was visiting someone in the countryside, stocking up on fruit for jams. We were rolling him back and forth between us on the bed—he was our doll, in a way—when he suddenly burst into tears, his body contracting into itself.

"Oh goodness, did something stick him?" I asked, frightened.

"No no, his stomach hurts, he's writhing," Adriana answered, trying to pick him up.

He calmed down after discharging a smelly liquid that dripped along his back to his neck. Adriana knew what to do: she took off his clothes in the bathtub and he stayed there on all fours, a pathetic defenseless puppy on the white, calcium-encrusted bottom. I couldn't touch him in that condition—I was disgusted in spite of myself—but she didn't need help, she washed him methodically, rubbing off the soft, foamy feces with her bare hands. She dressed him just in time for a second discharge that got everything dirty again and then again, until we had nothing else to put on him. So she wrapped him in a towel and held him as he howled, while she massaged his colicky stomach.

"It'll pass, it'll pass," she repeated in his ear, and to me, who was still in a daze, "Make him some tea and squeeze a lot of lemon into it," but I couldn't find anything in the kitchen and in my rush spilled water on the floor.

"Hold him a moment, I'll take care of it," but Giuseppe yelled loudly and wouldn't be separated from his more capable sister. "Go ask the lady downstairs." Adriana gave up.

The lady downstairs must have noted my desperate face and taken pity on me; she made the tea at her house. She came up with me to see and went back to get some old clothes of her children's. We put just a shirt on him; from time to time his intestine emptied again, though less violently. Now I could get near him; I dried his sweaty hair with a rag and finally he left Adriana for me.

The neighbor came back at noon, with a bowl of cream of rice for him. I fed him, and after a few spoonfuls he fell asleep in my arms.

"Don't you want to put him in the cradle?" Adriana asked, but it seemed to me that he was owed a sort of reparation, after what he'd suffered.

The muscles I was using to hold him went to sleep, like him, and when I moved a little they returned to feeling with a tingling sensation. I don't think I'd ever felt the pleasure of such intimacy with any creature.

When the mother returned she scolded us for some jobs we were supposed to do and hadn't, and for the floor that was still a little sticky in some places where Giuseppe had let go.

Later Adriana and I peeled peaches that would be preserved in syrup for the winter. She ate a lot of them, stealthily, so as not to be seen by the one who had brought them from the country-side. Dealing with the baby's diarrhea, we hadn't had lunch.

"Kids his age are usually walking already—he's still crawling, and he doesn't even say mamma," I observed, pointing to our brother, on all fours on the floor.

"Yeah, Giuseppe's not normal, hadn't you noticed? He's retarded," she said, matter-of-factly.

I stood with my knife raised, and the fruit fell out of my hand. Adriana's sudden, spontaneous summaries could be like thunderbolts. I went over to the baby crawling around the house; I picked him up off the tiles and held him in my arms for a moment, talking to him. From then on I saw him with different eyes, as his difference required.

I've never known exactly what he had, or what he lacked. Just a few years ago a doctor read me an abstruse diagnosis.

"Was he born with it?" I asked.

He considered me from head to toe, I think, with my proper outfit, my pleasing appearance.

"In part, yes. But other factors worked against him . . . environmental, let's say. As a child he must have suffered some form of deprivation."

He kept looking at me from behind the table, hands resting on the clinical chart. Maybe he was measuring the divide between my brother and me, and couldn't make sense of presumed "environmental factors." Or maybe that's my imagination.

In elementary school Giuseppe was one of the first children to have a teacher's aide, but there was a different person every year, and every June the bond was broken. I saw him leave a tear in the palm of his teacher Mimma's hand as a souvenir. He'd produced a great number of drawings since he was small, and drawing was his main activity in school. Hands were his favorite subject: he drew his classmates in the act of writing, paying particular attention to the fingers; the rest was just sketched, the head an oval with almost no distinctive features.

He never learned to defend himself, and if he happened into the middle of a scuffle by mistake he'd stand there, innocent and unmoving, exposed to accidental blows. No one ever hit him intentionally. One morning when I went to pick him up at school he had a cut on his cheekbone. The teacher explained that he'd been punched by a child who wasn't aiming at him. Giuseppe had grabbed the hand, opened it, and observed it for a long time, as if in search of the nexus between its beauty and the pain it had given him. The classmate had stood still, letting himself be studied.

17

T he bell rang. In the corridor the other students kept a distance that defined me as an outsider. Pasted to the desk where I was about to sit was an invisible label with the nickname people used in the town after I came back to the family. I was the *arminuta*, the one who was returned. I still knew hardly anybody. On the other hand, they knew more about me than I did: they'd heard the adults' gossip.

When she was a baby a distant relative wanted her for a daughter. But now she got to be a young lady why was she returned here to these losers? Did the woman who raised her die?

The desk next to mine remained empty, no one took it. The literature teacher introduced me as a child who'd been born there in the town but had grown up in the city and now had come back—I don't know who had told her.

"She'll be in the third year of middle school with you," Signora Perilli announced amid whispers and giggles. She asked a girl with crooked teeth to sit next to me; the girl obeyed, grumbling and scraping her chair noisily. "It will be good for you," the teacher added, when the surly girl finished settling herself and picking up the books she had dropped. "You'll be forced to speak some Italian." She was talking to her but looking at my face to see the effect of this first assignment she was giving me. Then she asked each of us how we had spent the vacation.

"I came here," I said softly when it was my turn. I left silent the moments she allowed me for continuing, and she didn't insist with questions. She had small, very blue eyes, and eyebrows so curved that they sketched almost perfect circles. From where I sat, in front and in the middle, I could see her clearly and smell her perfume. The slow flight of hands that accompanied her words through the air began to draw me in. During the second hour I noticed her legs, thickened by bandages that wrapped them under elastic stockings. She was very close, she placed her fingertips on my desk.

"I just had an operation on my veins," she answered my eyes alone.

With a start I raised my eyes as high as I dared, the teacher was right there. I paused at her jeweled rings, the mysterious lights in the secret depths of the colored gems.

"The blue is sapphire," she said, "and the red ruby. In geography we'll study the countries that produce these marvels." Then to the whole class: "Now we'll begin with a review of grammar. Starting today keep in mind that this year you'll take the exam for your middle-school diploma." She picked up a hairpin that had fallen out of her hair onto my notebook and returned to her desk.

She gave us some words to analyze, I answered the questions directed to the others, in a very low voice. She noticed and read my precision on my lips.

"What is *armando*, arming?" she asked.

"My uncle," some witty boy guessed.

"Very good, proper name of a person," she congratulated him, shaking her head slightly.

"And present gerund of the verb *armare*": it came out of me a little louder.

"The *arminuta* knows everything," Armando's nephew said, laughing.

"Yes, unlike you she has studied her verbs," Signora Perilli concluded curtly, shutting him up.

At recess Adriana appeared fearlessly at the door of the classroom. She had crossed the yard that separated the elementary school from the middle school and come to see how I was. Some buttons were missing from her blue smock and the hem had come unstitched and was hanging down. Any other child of ten would have appeared pathetic, so thin, hair greasy, in the midst of those bigger kids, immediately ready to make fun of her.

"What are you doing here?" the teacher asked, getting up in some alarm.

"I wanted to see if my sister's all right. She's from the city."

"Does your teacher know you left?"

"I told her, but maybe she didn't hear because the boys were making a racket."

"Then she'll be worried about you. I'll call a janitor who can take you back to your class."

"I can get back to the class by myself, I know the way. But first I'd like to find out if everything's O.K. for her here," and she pointed to me.

I had remained sitting in my place, paralyzed by shame. Red in the face I stared stubbornly at the desk, as if Adriana had nothing to do with me. I would have liked to kill her and at the same time I envied her that natural and bold unselfconsciousness.

Having been reassured by the teacher on my account, she raised her voice to arrange to meet me after school and then she left.

My classmates were all standing, scattered in small groups around the classroom. They were eating, talking and laughing—at me, I imagined. Adriana's visit made me an even easier target, or maybe I was exaggerating their interest.

I hadn't brought a snack, I wasn't used to making something for myself. From her desk the teacher observed me now and then, discreetly, paging through a book. In spite of her bandaged legs, at a certain point she got up almost suddenly.

"Eat this, at least. I always have some in my bag, for anyone who forgets to bring something," and she put a cookie on my desk. She moved away to an argument that was threatening to degenerate. After a few minutes she stopped again, on the way back to her desk. Recess was almost over. She asked me about Vincenzo, who had been a student of hers. I didn't know what to say, he hadn't been home for several days and no one in the family seemed to notice. Not even Adriana had a precise idea of where he was. And I, too, was beginning to forget about him a little.

"He works, but not all the time," I said.

The bell sounded and the others took their seats, with the usual scraping of the chairs' metal feet.

"What work?"

"Whatever turns up," and I saw him again one muggy afternoon splitting wood for a neighbor who was stockpiling it for the winter. I'd gone down to get something in the garage and was captivated as, without his knowing, I watched him, absorbed by the effort, every blow of the axe accompanied by guttural sounds. In the rotations of his upper body the muscles shone in the still crude light of day, a stream of sweat descended along his spine and wet his shorts.

"Too bad about school."

"What?"

"Too bad he left school," Signora Perilli repeated.

"He's a delinquent!" A voice from the back was raised.

She reached the boy who had overheard our brief conversation.

"I've also been told that you're a delinquent," she provoked him. "Should I believe it?"

On the way out I wanted to ignore Adriana, but it was impossible. She was waiting for me at the gate, joyful and skipping.

"You're a genius of verbs, the middle-school teachers are all talking just about you."

I kept going in silence. She always knew everything, almost before it happened, even today I can't explain it. She was always in the right place, hidden by a door, a corner, a tree, with her prodigious ear. She lost some of that ability as she grew up.

She was walking a few steps behind me, maybe humiliated by my sullen expression.

"What did I do to you?" she protested in front of the post office. The suspicion that she'd made me uneasy with her incursion into my classroom didn't even cross her mind. I decided to wait for her only when two boys from my class came up alongside her: I was the older sister and had to protect her.

"What are your parents, rabbits? Look at how many you are—six, seven now with the *arminuta*?" the bigger one teased her.

"At least our mother makes children with her husband, yours gives it to anyone who asks," Adriana replied promptly, as she took off. Just touching my arm she advised me to run, too, and so we escaped, aided by the element of surprise and our lightness. They didn't catch us, and when we felt safe we doubled over with laughter thinking about the fat-face who had gone pale at the insult.

"But what you said to him—what does it mean exactly?" I asked. "I didn't really understand."

"If you want to stay, you'd better learn the right verbs for around here, too."

18.

On an afternoon in October, after days of absence, Vincenzo returned, his face changed, with the look of someone who had passed a limit. He was wearing new clothes, and his hair, freshly barbered, exposed even more of the fish bone on his temple. He had brought a prosciutto, and he sat it down gently on a kitchen chair, like an important guest. With that surprise maybe he expected that no one would say anything about yet another of his flights. All eyes were fixed on the salted thigh, the bone sticking out of the dried meat. The father wasn't there, he hadn't come back from the factory.

"Shall we start now?" Sergio asked in that silence.

"No, we'll wait till it's time to eat," his brother answered brusquely.

He sent Adriana and me to the bakery, for a loaf of that day's bread. The mamma usually bought day-old bread, because it was cheaper.

The boys didn't dare leave, they stayed there, enduring, minute by minute, the long, nervous wait for dinner. Resting against the back of the chair, the prosciutto stared at us impassively. From time to time Vincenzo looked furtively at my body and at my face, doubtful about the origin of his gift to the family. Giuseppe crawled around the feet of the chair: even he felt all that attention focused on it.

"In the meantime let's cut it, why not?" Sergio said impatiently.

"No, he has to see it whole," Vincenzo replied fiercely, referring to his father, who was late.

Finally he arrived, on his pants splotches of unbaked brick, his fingers abraded and whitened.

"Your son came home with that," his wife said pointing with her chin. "Wash up, we're eating."

He gave a distracted glance at the dinner.

"Where'd he steal it?" he asked, as if Vincenzo weren't a few feet away, fists clenched, jaw grinding.

The father bumped into the chair as he was passing by to go and wash, and the prosciutto fell, with a soft thud. Sergio was quick to pick it up and put it on the table; he got a knife, the time had come. Vincenzo took the knife away from him, and headed toward the bathroom door.

"I'm working for a butcher down in the city, and the boss wanted to give me a bonus for my services, besides the money due," he said to his father as he was coming out of the bathroom, his hands wet. He pointed to the prosciutto with the knife blade and then brought it to his neck for a moment. "You talk shit because all you're good for is buying your children day-old bread from the baker," he hissed, before leaving him there, wordless.

He sharpened the knife against another blade and began cutting furiously. He tossed the slices onto a plate that Adriana held, shifting it this way and that so that he wouldn't miss the target, but her brothers' hands reached out to grab them almost in midair. I observed Vincenzo's skill in separating the skin from the fat with a blade so unsuited and felt guilty for my suspicions, like the father's. Maybe he really wanted to try to learn the job, and maybe the other time it wasn't a lie, either, that the Gypsies had paid him in gold. The town gossip might be baseless, too.

"Stop it, that's not the right way," he said to his brothers. "You have to eat it with bread, and you two aren't the only mouths."

At a nod from him the mamma understood that she should cut the bread. Adriana and I made sandwiches and passed them around several times, three or four each, but the first went to the father, who accepted it without embarrassment. Giuseppe sucked on a slice of prosciutto seasoned with the snot that dripped from his nose, until I saw him and cleaned it off. Adriana and I served ourselves last, along with Vincenzo. He had fed the entire family. He sat beside us and we ate in silence, while the others, now content, left the kitchen one by one.

"Signora Perilli says to say hello," I said at the end of the meal.

"Oh, her. She didn't want me to leave school."

"Actually she still thinks you should go back."

"Yeah, sure! Now I have a beard I show up with a notebook and make the kids laugh." He spoke with a swagger, but he blushed slightly.

"According to the teacher you're very intelligent."

"Well, I'm not going back, I have other stuff to do." He got up to put the prosciutto away; there wasn't much left.

"Now you're working in the city, you sleep at your friends'?" I asked, sweeping the crumbs up off the floor.

"So? What's the problem? The Gypsies I know live in houses, and they're good people, not like everybody thinks. The carabiniere put a lot of stupid shit in your head."

There was no moon at the window later, the room was in perfect darkness, and silent. I wasn't sleeping, but, perhaps distracted by my own breath, I didn't notice any movement, only, suddenly, the warm salty breath over me. He must have been kneeling on the floor. He moved the sheet aside and reached out his hand: I would never have imagined it so timid and light. But it was the beginning, or the fear that if he waked me abruptly I might cry out. I was immobile only in appearance, I had goose bumps on my skin, my heart was racing, parts of my body felt suddenly wet. From a distance I see myself again in my adolescent body, a battlefield between new desires and the prohibitions of those who had sent me back there. Vincenzo took my breast in his palm and found the nipple erect. I felt him move and the mattress yield beside me, but I didn't have a precise idea of his position. When he pushed his fingers on my pubis, I gripped his wrist with my hand. He stopped, but barely, and even I didn't know how long my resistance would last.

We weren't used to being siblings and we didn't believe it, completely. Maybe it wasn't because of our same blood that I resisted, it was a defense I would have tried with any other. We were breathing hard, suspended on the edge of the irreparable.

A yawn from Adriana saved us. Like a cat she was coming sleepily down the ladder in the dark to spend the rest of the night next to me. Certainly she had wet the bed above. Vincenzo moved rapidly and silently, an animal caught by surprise. My sister didn't notice him. I yielded to her a space warmed by energies she was ignorant of and she immediately started sweating. After a while she threw off the covers; I, too, continued to give off heat. I strained my ear toward Vincenzo's bed, I heard him tossing, then silence. He must have reached alone the place he wished to take me.

As on the other days I got up at dawn, to study at the kitchen table. Sometimes in the afternoon it was impossible, in that house. He, too, came in early, turned on the tap behind me and waited for the cooler water to come out. I heard him take a long drink, with big noisy swallows. I kept my head down over some war in the history book, but I had lost my concentration. He stayed behind me for a few minutes, I heard no movement. Then he came over to my chair, kissed my forehead after pushing aside the hair. He disappeared without a word.

19

The swirling script on the envelope that arrived in the morning belonged to Lidia, the sister of my father the carabiniere. On the side of the addressee she had written only my first name, the surname of the family to which it was to be delivered, and the town. She didn't know the exact address, but she hadn't put hers, either, where the sender's would normally go. Even without the street, the mailman delivered the letter, and the mother gave it to me when I came home from school.

"Don't think you're going to read it now, set the table," she ordered harshly.

She was irritated with me, in those days, after Signora Perilli had talked to her in the street. She had told her that I was a brilliant student and next year I would have to enroll in a high school in the city. She, the teacher, would supervise the decisions of the family in this matter and would go to the social workers if necessary. With that threat she had left her in front of the post office.

"She wants to come and take charge in this house, she says you mustn't end up like the boys. Did I force them to leave school?" the mother burst out. "And then is it my fault if you're too smart? You use up the light studying in the early morning and I say nothing."

After lunch she wanted me to wash the dishes, even though it wasn't my turn, and then she asked me to dry them. Usually they dried by themselves over the sink, but that day I was in a hurry to open the envelope and she made me waste time on purpose.

Lidia had written a simple note. From the folded paper some thousand-lire bills fell out. She had been told about my transfer, that's what she called it, and she was sorry, but I was a very intelligent girl and she had confidence in my ability to adjust. Unfortunately she was far away and busy with job and family, otherwise she would come and see how I was doing with my real parents. They aren't bad, she reassured me, they're our distant cousins, mine and your father's. I knew you were their daughter, but it wasn't up to me to tell you. And then I was sure you'd stay with my brother and sister-in-law forever. Sometimes it doesn't take much for life to change unexpectedly.

Some questions followed: perhaps she hadn't realized that having omitted her address she couldn't get an answer. She ended by saying that she looked forward to coming to see me in the summer, during the holidays. In the meantime the money might be useful for small personal expenses. She, too, was worried only about those, as if nothing else were missing where I was.

I stood with the page inert in my hands. An acid rage rose from my stomach, like a wave in reverse. The mother came over, attracted by the bills she had seen fall. She picked them up and handed them to me, and asked me to leave her a couple. I shrugged weakly, and she took that for a sign of assent. There was no one in the house at that hour. She leaned over to look for something in the area under the sink, among full or empty bottles, garbage can, cockroach dens. She closed the curtain over the odor of mold and turned. I was facing her, very close.

"Where's my mother?"

"Are you blind?" she answered, with a gesture toward herself.

"The other one. Will you make up your mind to tell me what happened to her?" and I threw Lidia's letter up in the air.

"How should I know where she is? I saw her once only, a little while before you returned. She came to talk to us, along with a friend of hers." She was panting faintly, sweat dampened the hair on her face.

"She's not dead?" I pressed her.

"Why would you think that? She'll live a hundred years, with the comfortable life she has," she said, laughing nervously.

"When she sent me to you she was sick."

"So, maybe, I don't know." The two thousand-lire notes that she had shoved in her bra had shifted and were sticking out of the V neck of her shirt.

"Then do I have to stay here forever or later on will they come and get me?" I ventured.

"You'll stay with us, that's definite. But don't ask me about Adalgisa, you'll have to deal with her."

"But when? And where? Will someone tell me?" I shouted at her face, so near mine.

I tore the rolled-up banknotes from her breast and ripped them to pieces. Astonished, she froze, and, unable to react immediately, couldn't stop me in time. She looked at me with fixed black pupils. She bared teeth and jaw, like a dog preparing to fight. The slap came cold, powerful: I swayed. A step in one direction, so as not to lose balance. I knocked into the bottle of oil she had taken from under the sink and it broke over the floor. For a few seconds we followed, hypnotized, the transparent yellow stain that spread slowly over the tiles, beyond the glass and over the fragments of paper money.

"It was half full and it was the last. This year you'll come, too, to pick olives. That way you'll learn what it is to earn what you eat," she said before starting to beat me around the head, which had caused the whole disaster.

I protected myself with my hands over my ears while she sought the exposed places where hitting would cause more pain.

"No, no, not her!" The cry came from Adriana, who had just returned with Giuseppe, I hadn't heard the door. "I'll clean it up now, you can't hit her, too," she insisted, stopping her mother's arm, in an attempt to defend my uniqueness, the difference between me and the other children, including her. I've never been able to explain the gesture of a child of ten who was beaten every day but wanted to preserve the privilege that I had, the untouchable sister who had just returned.

She got a shove that sent her to her knees on the oily glass. From the playpen Giuseppe joined her shrieks of pain. I helped her get up from the floor and sit, and I began to remove with my fingers the shards of glass sticking into her skin. Blood dripped along the downy hair that girls of that age sometimes have. We heard the door slam and the baby's crying suddenly cease, the mother had carried him off. For the tiniest fragments I had to use eyebrow tweezers that for some reason Adriana possessed. Some "ow"s escaped her, every so often. I also had to sterilize the wounds.

"Alcohol is all there is," she said, resigned.

When she cried because it burned, I cried, too, and asked her to forgive me, it was all my fault.

"You didn't do it on purpose," she absolved me, "but now seven years of misfortunes are coming. This is the first. Oil is like a mirror."

Finally I bandaged her knees with some men's handkerchiefs, we didn't have anything else. When she got up they fell to her ankles. She wanted to help me clean up, and we were careful not to cut ourselves. She saw the letter on the floor, and the torn bills, and I told her the story.

"You're always so quiet, today all of a sudden you have a fit?" she asked looking around the kitchen. "Did you at least hide the money you had left?"

The mother had placed it on the table when she picked it up, but it was gone. She must have grabbed it before she went out, in payment for the damage I had caused. She came back later as if nothing had happened, she was like that. She ordered us to peel the potatoes for dinner.

"The woman downstairs says you're the smartest in the school," she reported with a moment of pride in her usually apathetic voice, but maybe I only imagined it. "Don't ruin your sight with books, glasses are expensive," she added.

She never hit me again, after that.

20

We hadn't seen him for days. Gossip in the town said that he was with a gang of thieves who roamed the countryside and struck farmhouses, in different places at the same time, the rumor went.

The prosciutto he had brought was soon finished. The mother had sawed the bone into several pieces while Adriana and I held the ends. She had boiled them one by one with beans, and the soups were fat and flavorful. Our diet was unvaried for a while and our stomachs were upset.

My sister had a stomachache and didn't come to school that morning. The widow on the ground floor opened the door when she recognized my footsteps.

"Watch out, today something bad's gonna happen," she announced. "Last night two owls were singing outside the window of your mother's room," she responded to my questioning look.

When I came out of school the air was too hot for the season. I crossed the square between the market stalls that were being taken down. In front of the *porchetta* truck a gust of wind raised dust and paper, and the seller immediately covered the leftovers with a napkin. He saw me, as he did every Thursday.

"What are you doing here? You don't know about your brother?"

I shook my head no.

"An accident, the big bend past the dredge."

I stopped. I didn't want to ask which brother he was talking about. He added that our parents were at the place. I don't remember how I got there, who I asked to take me.

There were cars parked along the side of the road, behind the police car. Someone had called the police because of a robbery: people no longer trusted the carabinieri from the town, they never caught any of those troublemakers. The cops had chased the old motor scooter with the broken muffler, and at the bend, maybe on some of gravel or an oil slick, it had skidded off the road. The boy who was driving had held onto the handlebars and didn't have serious injuries, he was being operated on in the hospital.

Vincenzo had lost his grip around his friend's waist. He had flown over the autumn grass, as far as the cow pasture. Had he seen, in those few instants, what he was going to get caught on? He had landed with his neck on the barbed wire, like an angel too tired to beat his wings one last time, beyond the fatal line. The iron barbs had pierced his skin, cut open the trachea and severed the arteries. He was hanging with his head toward the grazing animals, his body limp on the other side, on his knees, one foot twisted. The cows had turned to look at him, then had lowered their muzzles and gone back to grazing. When I arrived, the farmer, inert, was supporting himself on the handle of his pitchfork, in the face of the death that had taken place in his field.

The police said they had to wait for the doctor. Leaning against a tree, I saw Vincenzo from a distance. I don't know why they hadn't covered him, he was exposed there to the curious, like a poorly made scarecrow. A light wind rose, now and then ruffling the edge of his shirt.

I crouched down, sliding my back along the roughness of the bark. From somewhere the mother's cries, like daylight howls. Then silence, occupied by a low voice that tried to console her. The father's curses rose to the sky, accompanied by arms threatening God. Other hands grasped his, attempting to calm him.

I lay down on my side and curled up in a fetal position on the tiny people of the grass. Someone noticed me, came over. The *arminuta*, they said, or: the sister. I heard them, but as if through glass. They touched a shoulder, my hair, grabbed me by the armpits and hoisted me up to sitting. It was impossible to stay on the ground like that. They described the accident to one another, sparing no details, as if I weren't there. They asked if the boys had been stealing. One swore they were, yes, but didn't know where or what. The police had found only two fishing rods, sent flying off the scooter, along with a bag containing some pike, caught at the river on that sunny morning. Maybe my brother would have brought them home for dinner, like the prosciutto. Two men marveled, they'd never seen such big ones around here.

The light alternated with the shadow of clouds coming from the mountain and a sudden cold. They wanted to walk me to the farmhouse, for a glass of water. I refused. After a while the farmer's wife came with a cup of milk from her cows.

"Take it," she said.

I shook my head, then something about her, the thickness of the hand on my cheek, persuaded me to try it. I drank a mouthful, but it tasted of blood. I gave her back the cup while the rain began to fall into it.

Vincenzo didn't come home: there wasn't room for a wake. The parish church received the rough fir coffin that held him, wearing the shirt and bell-bottoms he had recently bought. Out of pity the local doctor sutured the broad cut on his neck. The stitches resembled the iron barbs that had pierced his flesh at the end of his flight. That cut would not have time to become a scar like the fish bone on his temple. In the half-light, with its heavy odor of incense, his face appeared swollen and livid, except for some unexpectedly pale patches, with almost greenish tones.

Adriana had been the last to find out. She flung herself on her brother's empty bed, with a long outburst of tears.

"Now I can't give you back the money you lent me," she repeated to him in his absence.

Afterward she began to rummage through the rooms, feverish hands in drawers, in closets, in jars. I saw her hide something in a pocket, before she went out to join him in the church. The neighbors walked around the casket arranging next to his body objects that would be useful in Vincenzo's afterlife: comb, razor, men's handkerchiefs. Change to pay Charon for the crossing in the boat. Then Adriana went up to him, she touched the fingers crossed over his chest. She drew back suddenly, she wasn't expecting them to be so cold and rigid. She took the Gypsies' gift out of her pocket and wanted to put it on his middle finger, where he wore it. She couldn't, she had to unbend the pinky finger and it got stuck halfway. She rotated the ring slightly, to the side with the decoration carved in the silver.

Not many came to say goodbye to him, relatives of the family and old women of the neighborhood, whose only entertainment was going to see the dead. The teacher came and, instead of making the sign of the cross, like the others, stood beside him for a few minutes and then kissed him on the forehead.

The paternal grandparents, who never went anywhere, arrived from their mountain village. They sat beside their grandson, laid out forever. I didn't know them and I don't know if they remembered me as a newborn. Adriana told them in a whisper who I was, and from their immobility they regarded me for a moment, like a foreigner. They shrank into themselves. My first mother had already lost her parents and they couldn't comfort her.

Around eleven the priest began to put out the candles and

sent us all away. Vincenzo remained alone for his last night on earth, under the fixed stares of the statues.

I made out only a few words of the sermon the next morning, references to those who get lost for lack of a sure and steady guide, sheep gone astray whom the Lord would receive in his merciful embrace thanks to our prayers. As we came out there was a downpour and a circle of black umbrellas rose around us, in condolence. A stranger who didn't know what to say whispered good luck, kissing me on the cheeks. It must have been then that I felt I belonged to Vincenzo's family.

It wasn't raining at the cemetery. Few of us remained with him. At some point my father the carabiniere appeared on the other side of the grave, one hand holding the collar of his jacket up over his throat. He gave me a slight nod of greeting and then opened his mouth as if he wanted to speak to me from there. He closed it. He had a beard, as Nicola had told me, and looked a little scruffy. I barely reacted to that encounter, so long awaited: I didn't go over to him—at that moment I wouldn't have known what to ask. After a few minutes he'd already disappeared.

The Gypsies arrived, too, and they stood apart, where a shaft of sunlight poked through. There were four of them, I think my brother's age, except for one, who seemed more adult and wore a wide-collared purple shirt, with a mourning button pinned to the chest. They had polished shoes and brilliantine in their dark hair, combed back as on Sunday. Thus they paid homage to their friend, simply by their presence.

Beyond the boundary wall the horses waited for them, left free.

21

We went back to the cold house. That night snow appeared on the mountains, ahead of the season, and for several hours the wind whipped the valley. The windowpanes rattled in the rickety frames, drafts blew through the rooms. The neighbor, who had kept Giuseppe during the funeral, brought him back, but when she approached the mother with the child in her arms, the mother turned the other way. Not even Adriana wanted him. I took him, and sat down on a chair and leaned my head against the wall. I barely held him up, I had no strength. He felt that I wasn't reliable, and didn't move. The women from the other floors had prepared a funeral meal, food and drinks for us, on the table. I don't know if anyone ate.

After a while Giuseppe showed signs of restlessness, and wanted to get down. He crawled to his mamma, all in black, and looked at her from below with big, questioning eyes. Even from the depths of her despair she must have seen him. She went around him to go and lie on her bed, and she remained there until the following afternoon. The neighbors came to her in turn with a cup of hot broth, as when she had given birth, but she always twisted her lips.

In the following days we were invited to every meal by one neighbor or another. I preferred to stay and make do with something and bread or with what Adriana brought me from the neighbors' kitchens.

At night I thought I heard Vincenzo tossing between the

sheets, and so the death had been only a dream or a well executed trick. Sometimes it was his smell, so distinctive, spreading in the room. How harsh it was to return to the reality of his absence, afterward. His breath on my face even startled me awake, as when he had searched for me in the dark.

He wasn't the only one who occupied my hours of insomnia. At the cemetery I thought I had barely noticed my father, but his face, half hidden by the beard, returned, insistent. The eyes severe or, rather, disappointed. He had given up on the idea of speaking to me, I was sure of that. Maybe he was afraid that I would ask him to take me home again, or maybe there was more in his gaze. The weight of a silent reproach. And if he was the one who had decided to send me away? That was a possibility I had never imagined. But what could be my offense? Had he been told about a kiss in the school corridor? Too little to send a daughter away. I understood that, even though I was young, even in fantasies magnified by the night. If I had done something wrong, I didn't remember what.

At first the mother spent most of her time in bed, lying on her side with her eyes open. Giuseppe wanted to stay next to her, and he didn't bother her. The drops of milk that until a few days earlier he had still been able to suck from her breast had dried up. He stayed curled against her, in that passive heat. He climbed over the limp body, he wandered around it. After a few attempts to get her attention he stopped trying, it would have been useless. Sometimes, though, he wailed unexpectedly and I rushed in. Standing still for a few seconds in the room, I didn't know what to do. She looked at me with those eyes. So I picked up Giuseppe and took him away.

Then she began to get up, and the neighbors, finding her on her feet, stopped helping. But the mother did nothing in the house: as soon as she had enough strength she walked along the highway, as far as the road lined with cypresses. She always dressed in black and her uncombed hair was like leaves still attached to the branches of a tree in winter. One morning I asked if I could go with her, and she stared at me without responding. I followed her, a step behind; for two kilometers we didn't exchange a word. She came to life only on the ground that covered Vincenzo. Dead, he was the only child who counted for her.

On the way back I observed her, again walking ahead of me. I slowed down, fitting my pace to hers. The weeds along the embankment scratched her and she didn't feel them. Sometimes she strayed toward the center line, unaware of the danger. A honk made her jump, before I had time to correct her path. My pity suddenly turned to rage, inflamed me inside. There she was, the grieving mother of that reckless youth. She belonged completely to him, in his wooden box. She had nothing for me, who survived. Certainly when she gave me up, an infant of a few months, she hadn't been reduced to this. I caught up and passed her, I went on without turning back to see if she was safe from the cars. If someone was to protect her, it wouldn't be me.

Several days later, Signora Perilli rang at the entrance to the building, and asked for Adriana and me. We came down, ashamed to invite her into the house.

"Tomorrow you'll come back to school, both of you," she said imperiously. She added nothing else, her husband was waiting in the car with the motor running.

"I'll go back because I feel like it, not for her, she's not even my teacher," Adriana retorted on the stairs.

After school we had to cook something for everyone, usually pastina in broth. On my first attempts I put too little water in the pot or I overcooked the pasta, if my sister didn't pay attention to what I was doing.

"You're all head," she said discouragingly. "All you know how to do with your hands is hold a pen."

She was a skillful shopper, too, at the greengrocer she'd buy a kilo of potatoes and ask for carrots and onion for our vegetable broths. At the butcher barely two hundred grams of ground meat and some scraps for the nonexistent dog. We would boil those, too, but for us. Today I can't eat anything that might resemble our diet of that time. The mere odor of boiled meat makes me throw up.

"Keep track, at the end of the month Papa will come by," Adriana promised every shop owner. So quick and alert, with the bag in her hand, she disarmed them. Behind her, I was merely a mute reinforcement. The unease caused by the shopkeepers' brief glances as they served us, mouths shut, accompanied me out of the stores.

My sister was also fragile. She took refuge down on the ground floor, at the widow's. In exchange for company and a few tasks, she received affection and nourishment. She brought Giuseppe with her: "otherwise he'll die" slipped out one night when she came upstairs, carrying him half asleep.

The mother had lost her appetite and didn't think of ours. Returning from his shift at the factory the father sometimes brought some mortadella or salted anchovies, if the grocery was open. Otherwise he was satisfied with the pastina in broth that we prepared.

Some afternoons she sat in the kitchen, arms inert on the table. No one was there, at those hours. I cut some bread, rubbed oil on it, and moved the plate toward her, but not too close. I sat down, too, opposite, and began eating. I pushed the plate a little closer, just barely, with a finger. If she didn't feel forced, she might even take a piece and bite it, as if by reflex. She chewed slowly, like someone who is no longer used to it.

"It needs salt," she said at one of those moments.

"I'm sorry, I forgot it." I passed her the jar.

"No, it's fine without," and she finished the piece of bread she was holding.

More days of silence followed. She had again swallowed her voice.

One Sunday she saw me struggling with an onion for the vegetable broth.

"You always eat pastina in broth," she burst out. "Don't you know how to make sauce?"

"No."

"Put in the oil and fry it." We waited for the smell of the browning onion. She opened the bottle of tomato sauce we had prepared in August and I poured it in the pot. She instructed me on the height of the flame and the spices to add.

"I'll drain the pasta," she said later. "You're not practical, you'll certainly burn yourself."

I served the rigatoni with tomato sauce to the whole family and they seemed pleased to have a normal meal, but no one breathed. She accepted three or four pieces of pasta, without much sauce. She sat with the others, as when Vincenzo was alive, but she held the plate on her lap under the edge of the table and ate like that, head down.

22

The cream-colored Mercedes parked in the middle of the big square and was immediately surrounded by incredulous children. Two men got out, one with a mustache and the other in a broad-brimmed white hat. I saw them from the window, they asked a boy something and he pointed in my direction. They looked like Gypsies, and I was a little scared, but they didn't even ring the bell. They leaned on the hood of the car and waited, smoking. From time to time I checked on them without being seen.

When the father appeared at the end of the street, walking home from the factory, they threw the butts on the ground and moved toward him as if they recognized him. He merely slowed down and looked at them from a distance, then he headed toward the entrance, ignoring them. They barred his way and from his gestures I understood that the one with the mustache was talking first. I opened a window to listen.

"Gypsies don't enter my house. Tell me here what you want."

The acceleration of an engine muffled the answer, then again the father's voice, raised.

"If my son had debts with you, I don't know about it and I don't want to know. Go and get your money from him where he is now."

The closer one touched his arm as if to calm him, he gave him a push and the hat flew off, rolling white. Adriana had joined me at the window, we held our breath.

Nothing happened, the two men got back in the car and left, our father came inside, slamming the door.

Some days later they came up alongside us as we were leaving school, but the men weren't the same, and the car, which we saw only at an angle, seemed to us much smaller and was dented in several places. Adriana took my hand, and we joined some girls from her class. The men in the car followed us slowly as we walked along the sidewalk, then they passed us and, a short distance ahead, stopped to wait. After the square we were alone, the others had turned off. The boy who wasn't driving got out and came toward us with a half smile. My sister squeezed me with her sweaty palm, it was the agreed-on signal for an about-turn. That time she was the more frightened, she had heard stories about Gypsies who kidnapped children. We went quickly back toward the school, but at the corner where the tobacco shop was we practically embraced the man who was looking for us.

"Why are you running away? I don't want to bother you, just a question!"

He might have been twenty and close up he was more attractive than threatening. Even Adriana was reassured, she let go of my hand and with a gesture of her chin let him speak. Perhaps he felt awkward with two girls, his kindness was slightly forced. Had Vincenzo by chance left something for them, his friends? And maybe we were guarding it?

"But our brother certainly didn't know he was going to die. What would he have left?"

Adriana's brisk manner confused him. He described money lent for a scooter that Vincenzo wanted to buy. But he had it ready to give back, so he'd said a few days before the accident. Couldn't we look for it?

"He'd hardly have brought it home. He'd built himself a wooden hut down near the river somewhere and he hid his stuff there," the sly girl lied. Then she completed the work of

diversion with vague hints about the site of the hut. So we
freed ourselves from Vincenzo's creditors.

After lunch I saw her with an old shoe box under her arm.
She whispered to me to come down to the garage with her.

"The ring he's wearing in the afterlife was here," she said on
the stairs. "But there were other things. Now we'd better look
carefully."

We locked ourselves inside and I raised the lid on our
brother's secret world. A bunch of keys that weren't house
keys. A brand-new jackknife. A single sock, bulging because of
something it contained. I stuck my hand in, cautiously, and I
recognized the contents by touch. In front of Adriana's pale
face I took out a roll of bills held together with a rubber band.
There were all denominations, from ten to a hundred thousand
lire. Here was what the Gypsies wanted. Who knew if it was
really their money, or if Vincenzo had earned it with his odd
jobs and put it aside for the scooter.

With her fingertips Adriana tested the consistency of the
paper money—it must have been the first time she'd touched
a value different from the poor metal of the coins she sometimes got. She was enchanted.

"Who's this old man?" she asked, caressing the beard of
Leonardo on a fifty-thousand-lire note. She talked in a whisper, as if someone might be hiding in the trash around us.

"And now?" I asked her and myself. "It's too much, we can't
keep it."

"What do you mean? It's never too much," and she
clutched it, with a sort of spasm of her fingers.

Her excitement astonished me. That yearning in her eyes
on the bills. I wasn't acquainted with hunger and I lived like
a foreigner among the hungry. The privilege I bore from my
earlier life distinguished me, isolated me in the family. I was
the *arminuta*, the one who'd returned. I spoke another language and I no longer knew who I belonged to. I envied my

classmates in the town, and even Adriana, for the certainty of their mothers.

My sister began to imagine everything we could buy. The money lighted up her face from below, kindled a different appetite in her pupils. In the glow of the bulb hanging from the garage ceiling, I had to disappoint her as she dreamed on a scale too grand—a television, a polished tombstone for Vincenzo, a new car for our father.

"It's not enough," I said, touching her forehead as if she had a fever.

"It's impossible to understand you," she said impatiently. "Now it's too much, now not enough."

I saw her jump at a slight noise nearby, like something moving under a box. She pushed it with her foot and a thin tail disappeared behind a box of dried peppers.

"I knew it," she whispered. "See, we can't leave it here, or the mice'll eat it. Let's bring it back upstairs, but we have to stay on our guard, cause if Sergio finds it it's all over."

Toward evening the man from the funeral home showed up. In those days, we were often waiting for the head of the family to return. Without preamble, the corpse carrier, as everyone called him, demanded at least half the sum owed him for Vincenzo's funeral. Our father told him to be patient a little longer, it was possible that the factory would close, and the owners were months behind with the pay.

"The first money I get is yours, I swear it on my son," he said, but the other granted him only a week.

My sister and I listened with our heads down, avoiding each other's eyes. We were thinking of the next day, of the shopping we had planned. In the afternoon, when the stores reopened, we went out, lacerated by driving sleet. The urgent need for a coat for Adriana led us right away to the only clothing shop in the town, managed by a woman who looked like a potato with a head. Her arms, hanging along her body, could barely budge, and her short fat hands moved only if necessary. But the place was well lighted, and smelled of old dusty fabrics. The pleasant warmth of a kerosene stove welcomed us, whereas she examined us suspiciously.

"You're shopping by yourselves? Oh yes, you're the ones whose brother died, so your mother certainly isn't with you. Poor woman, always at the cemetery, no one would have expected it of her," she rattled off, all at once. "At least you have the money?"

Adriana crumpled up a Leonardo da Vinci virtually under her nose and then put it back in her pocket, neatly folded in half. Then we took our time choosing a forest green loden, of a generous cut.

"It has to fit when I go to middle school, too," my sister said to the shopkeeper, while she looked in the mirror, trying to see the big pleat at the back. She left her old coat there, inside out on the counter, with the lining that had come unstitched.

She walked home holding her feet stiffly in new loafers, so as not to ruin them. We were loaded with cheeses, packages of snack food, and doubts about how to explain the afternoon's purchases. We had found a wallet with something in it, that's what we'd say.

"I don't feel like hiding the food downstairs, let's eat it all at once," Adriana admitted.

No one asked any questions; the mother was always grieving and the father distracted by debts. The brothers merely gorged themselves on bread and Nutella that we put on a tray. I gave some spoonfuls to Giuseppe.

For a week we bought whatever we felt like, but the expenditures were always small, and mostly for sweets. The night the man from the funeral home returned we called to our father in the bedroom several times, and when he finally came out we put the money in his hands. So Vincenzo paid for his own funeral.

23

It was a week before the holidays. At lunchtime there were two crates of oranges on the bare table, something never before seen in that house. Next to them was a carton of cans placed one on top of another, some of tuna and most of meat. There must have been a late condolence visit that morning, while Adriana and I were in school. Besides the perfume of the citrus I smelled, now and again, another, but so light and uncertain it seemed a dream.

Giuseppe was sitting in a corner whimpering, he had bitten the skin of the fruit and it tasted bitter. From the bedroom the mother told us to open a can and be careful of the baby, she had gone to bed with a headache and hadn't cooked. A few days earlier she had resumed some of the household tasks, but every so often she would suddenly go back to bed and stay there for hours, her eyes open and empty.

I peeled Giuseppe's orange, starting from his bite mark, and gave him a section. He blinked and twisted his lips because of the bitterness of the juice, then he got used to it, tasting the sweetness, too, and wanted more. Adriana opened a can of meat and we ate it directly from the tin, taking turns fishing out forkfuls. Afterward she took the baby down to the widow's and I was alone. No sound came from the parents' bedroom.

There was no homework that afternoon, and I wandered from one part of the house to another, bored and restless. The color of all that fruit on the table. My seaside mother was obsessed with vitamin C, when I had a dance class she always gave me two peeled oranges to eat on the way, in the car. They're good for you before physical activity, she said. I went straight to the storeroom, gripped by a thought. I found the bag of mixed-up shoes I'd brought with me in August, and rummaged through it. My fingers picked out by memory the ballet slippers at the bottom, and in the kitchen I put them on under my checked skirt. The silk ribbons were a little dirty and frayed, my big toes hurt immediately, as they always did after the summer break. On my legs a lozenge of cold light from the window. I touched my instep, the unpracticed muscles of my calf. They were still there. Resting my hand lightly on the back of a chair I tried to go up on pointe holding fifth position, and I did a *battement tendu* ending in a plié.

"I told her you have to go back to the city for high school and those fine things." It was the mother, from the bedroom doorway. She spread her palm, as if in a gesture of admiration. "This morning Adalgisa was here and talked about you. But your father and I have been thinking about it ever since you came back, that know-it-all Perilli could keep her mouth shut. You're wasted here, nothing is right. In October next year you'll have to go to a good school. Adalgisa agrees."

It hadn't been a dream, the perfume that wasn't the oranges.

"So they'll take me back . . . " I ventured, in a voice that disintegrated in my mouth. I sat down. My legs felt unsteady, not because of the exercise.

"No, not that, but at the end of the summer she'll see about finding a place for you to stay in the city."

"Why did she come when I wasn't here? Couldn't she wait for me?"

"The lady who brought her was in a hurry. Adalgisa had heard belatedly about my poor son and wanted to visit."

"What do you mean belatedly, if my father was at the funeral?"

"Obviously your uncle didn't tell her," she corrected me.

"Odd. How is she?"

"Oh, not bad," she answered quickly, turning three-quarters of the way around. "Did you see how much stuff she had delivered? It's time to find a place for it." And she began putting the cans away in a cupboard. So she closed herself up again in her usual reticence on the subject. My questions no longer reached her. She talked to herself in an undertone, a habit she'd developed since she'd begun recovering, slightly, from Vincenzo's death. She asked the cans what was in them, the shelf how high it was, she'd never reach it, and her poor son where he was at that moment.

I stayed sitting on the chair, I didn't help her. A fierce rage was starting to swell in my stomach. At first, it sapped my strength, sucking the blood from every vein. I took off the pointe shoes, struggling like a tired old lady. I stroked the satin for a moment, sniffed inside searching for the carefree odor of the feet of another time. Suddenly, a destructive energy pervaded me, as if I'd had an injection whose effect was instantaneous. I laid my right hand on an orange, the first available object in the world. It was soft in one place, rotten. Savagely I sunk my fingers into the center and past it, toward the peel on the opposite side. My hand trembled, along with the fruit, and its color of distant sunshine. The juice dripped, wasted, along my wrist and wet my shirt. I don't know how long after that I threw it blindly at the wall: it passed a few centimeters from her head. She didn't even have time to turn before I shoved the crate, which was still on the table, and the fruit fell and rolled every which way over the floor.

"Are you crazy? What's got into you?"

"I'm not a package, you all have to stop moving me here and there. I want to see my mother, now you tell me where she is and I'll go by myself." I stood up, shaking.

"I don't know where she is, not in the house where she was before."

I moved closer, trapping her between me and the sink. I grabbed her by the black-clothed shoulders and shook her roughly.

"Then I'll find a judge and report all of you. I'll tell him you exchange a daughter like a toy."

I ran outside and stayed there; soon darkness fell and chilled me. From the most secluded corner of the big square I saw the windows light up and, behind them, the coming and going of busy female silhouettes. In my eyes they were normal mammas, those who had borne children and kept them. At five in the afternoon they were already absorbed in the preparations for dinner, the long-cooking, elaborate dishes that the season demanded.

In time I lost that confused idea of normality, too, and today I really don't know what place a mother is. It's absent from my life the way good health, shelter, certainty can be absent. It's an enduring emptiness, which I know but can't get past. My head whirls if I look inside it. A desolate landscape that keeps you from sleeping at night and constructs nightmares in the little sleep it allows. The only mother I never lost is the one of my fears.

That night Adriana came to look for me. There had been two flashes of lightning and the obscurity of the big square frightened her. She stood near the doorway and called into the darkness. Resisting her pleas, like a lost cat's, was painful, but I tried. I glimpsed her, she, too, had come down without a coat, she stamped her feet and rubbed her arms to get warm. Go, go back, I begged her from inside myself. Or, more secretly: wait for me, wait till I'm ready. She heard me, and answered it all, aloud.

"If you don't come back, I'll stay here and get sick because of you. My nose is already running."

I waited a little longer before giving in to her. Then I moved under a working light and she saw me. She ran to hug me.

"That crackbrain . . . " she said, rubbing my wet back. "When you get it in your head to run away, don't you think about me?"

I wasn't hungry, I went right to bed. Through the closed door I heard the voices in the kitchen. Then someone came into the bedroom and I pretended to be asleep. It was the mother. I recognized her from the way she dragged her slippers. She must have known that I was awake.

"Put this on your chest, otherwise you'll get a fever," and she moved the covers aside.

She had warmed a brick in the oven and wrapped it in a rag so that it wouldn't burn me. Well-being slowly spread under the weight, to my heart. It beat more calmly.

She must have left silently, while I succumbed to a brief, deep sleep. I didn't get a fever.

24

I realized it was Christmas because of the school vacation and the bells ringing continuously at midnight. I heard them from my bed: we hadn't gone to Mass and hadn't had a special Christmas Eve fish dinner. We'd had *pane cotto*, escarole and beans, but I liked it better than the stewed eel of other years. I'd always found the eel gluey, but had to eat some out of respect for tradition, as my mother wanted.

In the morning the neighborhood women remembered the recent bereavement and they came over with something for Christmas lunch, *brodo di cardo e stracciatella*, broth with eggs, baked crepes with meatballs, turkey *alla canzanese*, in aspic— all the traditional dishes of the area. On the evening of the twenty-fourth, the owners of the brick factory decided to pay the workers at least one of the paychecks they were owed, so our father went to the grocery store and bought two boxes of nougat. When we finished the meat we divided them in pieces and nibbled on them, sitting at the table longer than usual. Adriana was the greediest and she chewed noisily. Suddenly she screamed and jumped up, clutching her jaw. I followed her into the bedroom, where she had run to cry.

She opened her mouth and with her index finger touched a half-blackened baby molar. A pale splinter was stuck in the central hollow, maybe a sliver of almond, and had reignited the pain she'd been having sporadically for a while. To get out the fragment of candy Adriana dug into the cavity with a toothpick she kept in her pocket, then she held up the tip to my nostrils.

"What a stink—smell it. That stupid thing won't come out, you get it, I can't do it this time."

I was afraid I'd hurt her, but she insisted. The tooth seemed attached to the gum just in one place, but it hardly moved, its time hadn't yet come. I tried to push it with my fingers, nothing happened. Not even with a thread around it: when I tugged I got an empty noose.

"You need a tool," she suggested.

We looked in the kitchen. The others had gone, the table had been cleared, only the pile of dirty dishes awaited us in the sink. I opened some drawers without a definite idea, examining the most disparate objects. Not a knife, it scared me. A fork. We went to the window, toward the winter sun that was already setting. Adriana opened her lower jaw to me. I placed one of the tines where it looked as if the tooth was beginning to detach. She was motionless and quiet, her arms suspended midair. When I inserted the point deeper I looked into her eyes to lighten the pain. Her pupils dilated, nothing else moved. Holding my breath, I used the fork as a lever, suddenly. The tooth shot out into her throat, while a ribbon of blood erupted from her gum. Between coughing and uttering strangled sounds Adriana got rid of the foreign body, spitting it into the palm of my hand; a red wake followed. Then she sucked up the saliva and plugged up her mouth with a rag.

That night I cried into my pillow. Who would take out her baby teeth when I returned to the city? She heard me and came down. I told her about the most recent encounter of my two mothers, a week before, and about the new move they had decided for me.

"So now you'll go away?" Adriana asked, dismayed in the incomplete darkness.

"Not now, when high school starts, in September."

"And isn't that what you wanted?" she asked after a pause.

In her suddenly adult tone a hint of reproach, but slight, affectionate. "They forced you to come back here, and you don't like it. Ever since you returned you've cried every night, you toss under the covers, you don't sleep. And now you're not happy to go back to the city?"

"I'm not sure about anything anymore, it's all confused. No one tells me where I'm going. My mother will make some arrangement for me, maybe a boarding school."

"Is she crazy? In boarding school the nuns are in charge, and they're terrible, they even check your underpants."

"What do you know about it?"

"There was a girl who lived behind the bakery. The stories she tells!"

"It's not so much the nuns I'm worried about," I murmured, touching her hair. "I won't see you anymore," and I started sobbing again.

We were both disconsolate for a while, then she jumped up and sat on the bed.

"The two of them send you from place to place whenever it occurs to them. That's enough, you have to rebel," she urged, shaking me by the shoulder.

"How?"

"Right now I don't know, I have to think about it. Meanwhile let's swear not to ever leave each other. If you go, I'll come with you."

She crossed her index fingers and kissed them on both sides, turning over her hands with a rapid motion. I glimpsed her in the dim light. I swore as she had.

I hugged her and she immediately fell asleep, her back against my chest, her vertebrae like beads of a rosary. When she wet the bed I stayed still, clinging to the warmth that bathed my stomach. Every so often she jerked, at one point she even laughed, I have no idea what she might have been dreaming. On other nights her body relaxed in sleep calmed me, but not this one. My anxieties weren't for myself and my uncertain future—I transferred them to Adriana and Giuseppe. So I tamed them. Already, a few minutes after making that promise, I no longer believed that we would stay together. In September I would leave the town alone. How could those two manage without me? She might make it, but the baby? He was still crawling and I had never heard him say mamma or papa. To help him, I uttered slow syllables, exaggerating the movements of my lips, but his attention wandered. He wasn't ready.

At the institution where he lives now, there is one aide he talks to, always the same one, and when that aide goes on vacation he's silent. So they tell me.

On every visit I bring him pads of paper and pencils of all different degrees of hardness, he looks at them and feels the points with his index finger, one by one.

"They're good," he says. And then, serious: "Here are the works for this month."

Usually he draws his hands as they are drawing themselves, the right at work and the left holding the paper steady. But also animals running, dogs, or horses galloping, caught at the moment when no hoof is touching the ground.

Nevertheless, Giuseppe was the only one of the brothers to finish middle school, and then he spent some years at home, increasingly mute and distant, on the far edges of everything that happened. The place he's in now is better for him. It was once a convent, and when the weather permits the residents spend many hours of the day in the sunny garden.

Usually Adriana comes with me, and fills the hour with chatter. When I go by myself we sit silently on a bench for a long time. Sometimes Giuseppe gives me a leaf, if one falls nearby.

In spring I bring him a basket of strawberries, we wash

them in the fountain beside the hedge. Then he eats them, after holding them up to the light, one by one, gripping them by the stem. He observes the tiny variations in shape, in color. I suspect that he's trying to count all those seeds on the surface.

25

The winter was long and harsh, and at home we were freezing. In the early morning I studied under the covers—the widow on the ground floor had given me a lamp that I kept next to the bed—and my numb fingers struggled to turn the pages. In March I won a school contest with a paper on the European Community, and the teacher gave me a savings book in my name, from the Ministry of Education. Then she turned to the class: "You can be proud of your classmate," and with the weight of her gaze on the students who usually made fun of me, she insisted. "Only twenty students in Italy received this prize."

"And one is the *arminuta*," a mocking voice burst out predictably at the back of the room.

By the end of the school day my sister already knew about it, I had no idea how, and she ran ahead to report the news to the family. She showed the book to our parents, all excited. It was red, and inside, handwritten in the column for deposits, it said thirty thousand lire.

"Can that be taken out of the bank?" the mother asked, after reading it. She closed the book and put it on the table, but she continued to stare at it.

"That can't be touched," the father said, surprisingly. "It's hers, she earned it with her head," he added after a pause.

"She also got ten in math, she likes doing the problems," Adriana added, circling them.

I liked the solid geometry of that year, the complex figures, pyramids superimposed on parallelepipeds, cylinders with cone-shaped holes dug into one base. I really enjoyed calculating surfaces and volumes, adding and subtracting them in search of the total. But then I thought that those excellent grades were propelling me straight toward the tomorrow that the two mothers had planned for me in my absence. And I wasn't sure I wanted to follow the direction they'd chosen. The next winter I would be going to a high school in the city, but where would I eat, sleep? Would Patrizia and I be able to meet in the afternoon? Sometimes rather than that uncertainty I thought that I would have preferred to stay where I was, with Adriana and Giuseppe, and the parents who had taken me back, and even Sergio and the other boy.

The teacher returned my Latin homework with a nine on the back of the sheet of foolscap, and, after a moment of joy, I felt lost as I looked at it lying on the desk. My mother would indeed have been pleased, if she could have seen it. She still worried about me, albeit from a distance, more than she worried about her illness: I refused to stop believing that. And yet, in certain melancholy moods, I felt forgotten. I'd fallen out of her thoughts. There was no longer any reason to exist in the world. I softly repeated the word mamma a hundred times, until it lost all meaning and was only an exercise of the lips. I was an orphan with two living mothers. One had given me up with her milk still on my tongue, the other had given me back at the age of thirteen. I was a child of separations, false or unspoken kinships, distances. I no longer knew who I came from. In my heart I don't know even now.

My birthday fell in the spring and no one was aware of it. The parents had forgotten in the time that had passed without me, and Adriana didn't know the date. If I had told her she would have celebrated in her way, jumping up and down and pulling my ears fourteen times. But I kept it a secret and told myself happy birthday, as soon as midnight struck. In the afternoon I went up to the square and bought a *diplomatico* in the only pastry shop in the town. I asked for a small candle, the kind you put on a cake. The woman looked at me strangely and wouldn't let me pay. Thus, I got a present.

In the garage I found matches right away—I knew where they were. I locked myself in, and, in the faint light that came through a kind of peephole, I took the pastry out of the bag and placed it, with the bag underneath, on the dusty surface of an old credenza. I stuck the candle in the middle of the pastry and lighted the wick. In the almost black half light there were no points of reference and I could believe in a real cake, of normal dimensions. I stood watching the flame, which quivered slightly, maybe because of my breath on it. I wasn't thinking of anything precise, but, besides my fears, I had inside me a luminous force like that small fire. The liquefied wax began to drip along the solid part, down to the powdered sugar. Then I blew it out with a puff and solitary applause, and I sang "Happy Birthday," whispering in the darkness. The *diplomatico* was fresh, flaky, I ate it down to the last crumb. Then I went upstairs.

That night a man came to invite us to the country the following day, Sunday. It was already late, and he sat with our father at the kitchen table. He looked like a pirate, because of a black patch over his right eye, held on by a string that circled his head, which was almost bald, except for some curly gray tufts on his neck. In one corner of his mouth he balanced the butt of an old cigar, the tip blackened by previous smokes. He never took it out, so when he spoke he twisted his jaw to that side. I was curious about him and a little frightened by his appearance.

"At this hour your wife is already in bed," I heard him say. "She still hasn't recovered from the tragedy, of course. Tomorrow, you'll see, some fresh air will help and then there's

Nonna Carmela who wants to see her again, she's always thinking of her goddaughter. She gave me this for her, you stick it
under the mattress, where she puts her head."

I only glimpsed the object, which looked like something
wrapped in fabric. Our father put it in his pocket and got up
to get a bottle of wine; Adriana and I couldn't reach the cupboard where it was kept.

"And whose child are you?" the pirate asked me point-
blank when he noticed that I was new there.

"She's my sister," Adriana immediately broke in. "They
gave her to a cousin, when she was a baby. Now we've taken
her back."

"I'd heard that fact. So tomorrow you'll come, too, at my
house we have everything," he encouraged me, examining me
with his single eye.

Later, from the top bunk, Adriana told me the story of the
man with the eye patch. He was a godfather of ours, who lived
in a place where all the land was farmed. When he was a boy a
rock tossed up at full speed by the tire of a maneuvering trac-
tor had hit him in the right eye, blinding him. Because he
always had the cigar stub in his mouth he was known to everyone as Half-Cigar, but you got in trouble if he heard it.

"What's his real name?" I asked.

"I don't remember, but anyway in the country you have to
call all the grown-up men uncle even if they're nothing to you,
that's the custom."

"What did he give him for her?" And I leaned out to point
to the parents' room.

"I don't know, maybe a talisman. His grandmother is really
old and she's a folk healer. People go there to get advice and
medicines. When I had whooping cough she sent me a syrup
that was really disgusting, I kept spitting it out. And for worms
she uses wood, oh Lord how bitter it is!"

I discovered only years later that Adriana's "wood" was

wild wormwood, whose curative properties were known to the country healer.

We left the next morning, in the slightly uncooperative car. The brothers didn't come: You always have to work in the country, they said, and they didn't feel like it. Adriana didn't usually get carsick, and yet she began to complain of nausea as soon as we left the town, maybe she had drunk some milk right at the last moment. We stopped just in time at the bend beyond the dredge, and she threw up her breakfast on the edge of the field that had drained Vincenzo's blood. There it was, the fence that had ended his flight.

I stood next to my sister while she was throwing up. The mother didn't get out, instead she closed the window and turned in the other direction with her hands over her face. From the movements of her shoulders in the car I could see that she was sobbing.

26

At the farmhouse we were greeted by the scent of flowering acacia and a numerous family, of several generations. They were all in the farmyard, engaged in various activities. Half-Cigar was sharpening a scythe, rhythmically pounding the edge of the blade with a big hammer. He seemed really pleased to see us. Maybe he had talked about me; no one was surprised by my presence, only they looked at me with curiosity, especially the children. Two boys were taking the sheep to pasture, but they sent them on ahead with shouts and whistles and stopped to greet us. The wife left a bucket of grain for the chickens and went inside to get something for us to drink. The men had anisette, for us women and children she had a sour-cherry drink bottled the year before.

"You'll take some bottles later," she said, and, more softly, to our mother: "Nonna Carmela is expecting you, you know where she is."

She took Giuseppe gently from her arms and pointed with her chin toward an ancient oak beside the house. I followed the mother in that direction, without understanding. A short distance away I saw her and stopped abruptly. She occupied a high chair with a roughly carved back, a sort of rustic outdoor throne. She was wearing a big smock buttoned in the front, the color of the shade that sheltered her. I stood there staring at her, enthralled by her fairy-tale grandeur. The skin of her face, burned by the sun of a hundred summers, blended into the bark of the tree behind her: it had the same immobility, the same texture of cracks. To my eyes both appeared timeless, the old woman and the oak.

They told me later that she had died once and remained dead for several days, but she couldn't bear the solitude and had returned.

"Godmother Carme' . . . " the goddaughter called, her voice already breaking.

"I know it all, my girl, I know it, how you feel," and she summoned her close, with a very slight gesture of her arm. At every movement I heard creaks, groans, the contractions of rusty joints.

The mother knelt beside her in tears and placed her head in her lap, her cheek facing up. A broad, ancient palm arrived promptly to cover it.

"For the illness you have, there's no medicine I can offer," she confessed without guilt. She raised a hand for a moment, looking at it in its impotence, then she brought it down to give what she could, a rough caress.

"Hello," I said, out of politeness.

She stared at me, focusing, but her eyes were almost completely covered by the drooping lids, and all I could distinguish was two narrow cracks through which penetrated what she could still know of the world. A small girl came running with a bunch of newly picked herbs.

"Are they good?" she asked, breathlessly.

"There's still the dew on them?"

Yes, they were damp with dew. So they were good. The great-grandchild put them in a glass on a low table I hadn't noticed, also in the shade of the oak. On the tabletop were bottles and jars containing strange concoctions and poultices, of all kinds and for all spells. Also an oil cruet and a dish of water, to drive out and cure the evil eye. A small knife with which she drew signs on the body corresponding to the diseased organs, but without cutting.

Just then a car arrived and two people got out, in search of advice and remedies from Zi' Carmela.

The mother rose. The old woman spoke to her.

"You were born under a bad planet, but this one will bring you success," she said, shaking a finger at me.

Then she received clients for hours, sometimes a line formed, there in the farmyard. They were taking advantage of the waning moon, the most propitious phase for reducing all evils, Half-Cigar's wife explained to me.

It wasn't true that we had to work that day, we had only to pick favas in a field and eat them at lunch. They gave us baskets and we went; Giuseppe stayed in the house with a little girl who adored him. We were accompanied by a clamor of birds, swallows darting incessantly over our heads. They were carrying insects to the newborns waiting in nests attached to the beams of the barn. We skirted a field of barley, with its sharp hairy spikes. As I passed I grazed blades of grass limp in the insistent sun; its rays dazed me, after all that winter. There was the garden, with straight, parallel furrows, and in the hollows salad heads at regular intervals; and the plot set aside for tomatoes, the plants still young and fragile.

We reached the favas. I picked the first pod so clumsily that I bent the thin stalk to the ground. I looked at it, mortified.

"Come here, I'll show you how to do it," the mother said. "Hold it here at the top with one hand and pick with the other."

I stayed beside her, we used the same basket. The others were a little farther on.

"Try them, they're good," and she filled my fist with beans. They tasted of green, of morning sap, little creatures that you were almost sorry to crush between your teeth.

We kept on with our harvest. Here and there amid the leaves were lumps of whitish foam. It was the spit of the cuckoo, she explained, and Godmother Carmela used it sometimes in her potions. Only recently I happened to read that it's produced by the larva of the spittlebug, and the fable dissolved.

"Everything here is so well tended, so orderly," I said with a sigh. "I wish my life were like this field": the words slipped out.

Maybe the place invited intimacy, maybe it was the influence of the healer.

The mother didn't answer, but she was listening.

"How old was I when you gave me to your cousin?" I asked softly, wearily but without anger.

"You were six months old, I was weaning you. After she brought the traditional gift of money, which is supposed to encourage sleep, Adalgisa returned every week, she always wanted to take you back to her house."

"Why?"

"For years she'd been trying to have children and couldn't."

Nearby the others were picking and eating, at times the squealing voice of Adriana reached us, followed by laughter.

At first my mother refused, but then she got pregnant with her fifth child and my father lost his job. They had talked one night, shut in their room, while I was sleeping unaware in the cradle and my brothers were sleeping, too, in the other room. They had given in.

The cousin wanted me specifically, small and a girl; otherwise love wouldn't develop. She took me before I could understand.

"She didn't take anything with her from our house, she bought everything new. I kept your things for the child in my womb, but after twenty days I lost it. I bled and nearly died."

"You couldn't come and take me back?" I asked weakly.

"Adalgisa wouldn't give you back, she was already raising you, as she said."

I sat on the ground, with my chin on my knees. My eyes were burning with the effort to hold back tears. She remained standing, with the full basket hanging on her arm. It must have been midday, she was sweating in silence. She couldn't take that one step that separated us from consolation.

From the farmyard they called us for lunch. We came in from the field, all heading in the same direction on the path that separated the crops. Free of the danger of our feet, the plants became neighbors.

"Why such serious faces?" Adriana asked, all cheerful.

A long table awaited us, set under an awning. And warm bread to eat with oil and raw favas; cooked favas with new onions, pecorino cheese, prosciutto from a pig sacrificed the year before. On a grill sheltered from the wind, lamb was already cooking on skewers. My father talked to Half-Cigar, they drank wine from the previous harvest, praising its strength and color. Maybe I had never seen him laugh so much: only then did I notice his missing teeth.

The old woman didn't move from the shade of the oak; they brought her some food there, though she didn't eat much now, and no meat. During our long lunch she continued to receive people, healing them with poultices and ancient, secret words.

She died at a hundred and nine, sitting in her usual place. A sort of flame rose from her last breath that instantly dried the foliage of the tree, leaf by leaf. That was how they realized almost immediately that she was no longer there. Three days after the funeral, the monumental trunk fell to the ground, with a nighttime crash that woke the entire district. On the right side, though, without hitting the house. For years it provided wood for Half-Cigar's family to burn, and, who knows, maybe it still burns during their winters.

27

We were playing in the big square, around noon. Ernesto's son came running to tell me that at four in the afternoon someone would telephone me at the wine shop. He hadn't spoken to the person in question and didn't know who it was. I immediately began to imagine the person in question, and that took away my appetite for lunch, beans with potatoes.

That morning I had been at school with my mother, to collect my middle-school diploma. As always since Vincenzo's death, she was dressed in black, in a shapeless skirt and a shirt faded from washings. Among the results posted in the corridor I had read her my "EXCELLENT" and she was utterly matter-of-fact. She thought everything came easily to me, she didn't know how I had suffered over the Latin test, with that pair of *auts* so far apart as to blind me to the obviousness of the meaning. In the second hour the teacher, passing by the desk, had twice formed her lips into an "or," and the tangled skein of the translation had immediately been freed from its spell.

The moment we entered the classroom where the diplomas would be handed out, I felt my mother's hand cross my back and stop decisively on my shoulder blade. I'd sunk my head down between my shoulders, like a dog fearful and pleased by the first caress after long neglect. But I escaped quickly, with an abrupt movement, and pulled slightly away. I was ashamed of her, of her cracked fingers, the faded mourning, the ignorance that slipped out at every word. I never stopped being ashamed of her language, which, when she tried to speak properly, became a ridiculous dialect.

The public phone booth was at the back of Ernesto's shop, in the sun. A stale smell of cheap wine was strong there, along with the blurred conversations of the old men who were drinking it even at that hour, in that heat. I arrived early, and waited for the call sitting on an old stool that swayed every time I moved. I jumped up at the first ring. Ernesto answered and handed me the line. I was afraid to pick up the receiver and hear her again, after all that time. I closed and immediately reopened the door of the booth, I was suffocating. I delayed a few more seconds, thinking that I had to hurry, or she would hang up, maybe forever. I said hello and breathed into the little holes of the receiver.

I imagined that she would be moved, but no, she wasn't. She greeted my ear and asked how I was, with only a slight hesitation.

"How are *you*?"

"Thank God. But tell me about you, instead."

She quickly broke the silence that followed.

"I hear that you're the best in your school, I expected it."

Her capacity for getting information at a distance was surprising. In the classroom just a few hours earlier, at the end of the brief ceremony at which the diplomas were handed out, Signora Perilli had spoken to my mother.

"Your daughter was the best, she has a real talent for studying. And now you mustn't waste it, we already discussed it, remember?" she had asked, staring at her. "Here are the names of three high schools in the city. Consider them and then let me know where you're thinking of enrolling her. If it's all right with you I'd like to stay informed about her academic progress," she had concluded, handing my mother a sheet of paper.

For me, on the other hand, she carried books for summer reading in her bag. Finally she had held my face in her hands like something precious and kissed my forehead. One of her rings got tangled in a lock of hair and when she managed to free it a hair remained twisted around the amethyst from Brazil. I said nothing, and so a tiny part of me would stay with her a little longer.

At the door my mother had had a second thought and she turned back.

"I didn't go to school, but I'm not stupid, professor. I understood on my own that she has a brain for studying." She touched my head as she spoke. "I'll see how I can arrange things and I'll have her go on."

The voice in the receiver was a little different from the last time, fuller and rounder, even after it had traveled all those kilometers of cables. It didn't sound sad, nor was there any hint of illness. For an instant I believed that she was well and ready to take me back. Was that why she was calling? A blade of anguish unexpectedly pierced my throat at the prospect of what was, for me, more desirable. I no longer knew what I desired. It was only a moment of confusion; meanwhile the other continued, calmly.

"Maybe your mother already told you that we want to send you to a good high school—you deserve it."

It was chilling the way the subject of that sentence came to her so spontaneously, as if she, too, were not my mother but a wealthy old aunt willing to pay for my future.

"So I'll come home? In the town there's no high school," I ventured after a pause.

"Actually I thought of settling you at the Ursulines, it's a very good girls' boarding school. I would take care of the expenses."

"Forget boarding school. I'd rather not go to school anymore," I replied curtly.

"Let's see if we can find another solution, then, maybe a reliable family would take you as a boarder."

"But why can't I come home with you? What did I do to you?" I almost shouted.

"Nothing, I can't explain now. But it's very important to me that you continue your studies."

A boy came over to the booth and walked back and forth impatiently. I closed the door suddenly, pulling on the vertical handle.

"What if Patrizia's parents would take me?" I challenged her.

"They don't seem to me like the right family. But don't worry, we have plenty of time to get organized."

A sound in the background, as of a chair moved. Then a male voice that said something. But I wouldn't have been able to swear to it, there was occasional interference on the line.

"Who's there with you, Papa?" I asked, my whole body in a sweat. The boy knocked on the rectangle of glass and tapped his wristwatch several times with his index finger.

"No, it's the television," she said. "By the way, I thought of giving you one, I think you don't have one there."

"Will you two come and bring it?"

"I can't, I'll have it delivered."

"Then save your money, I don't want it. Since you've decided that I'll leave in September, right? And in the summer we're always out in the street, we won't watch it."

I was hoping to provoke her but she didn't react. She was in a hurry now, more than the kid who was marching back and forth in a huff outside the phone booth. Again the voice in the background, but I couldn't understand the words. And then a strange sound. She promised to call me back, and we would also meet, she said. She ended with a hurried goodbye and hung up, without waiting—in vain—for mine. I stood with the sweaty receiver in my hand and an intermittent beep, in my head a flammable rage. I immediately decided not to see her again, and no more "mamma," even inside I would call her Adalgisa, with all the ice that the name concealed. I truly lost her, and for a few hours I thought I could forget her.

"Look who it was, the *arminuta*," the boy said when I came out. He spat as he looked at me.

"Take your time on the phone while I go get my brothers. They'll rip you to pieces," I threatened through fiercely clenched teeth.

In the middle of the afternoon I was combing Giuseppe's hair with my fingers, and he was still and quiet on my bed: he liked that. How could I know the effort she had made not to cry, hearing me after almost a year. Or maybe for a few seconds she had had to cover the mouthpiece with her hand, I knew that gesture. If she still wasn't able to take me back, there were surely serious reasons that it wasn't the moment to explain, that's what she'd said. Basically girls like me couldn't understand everything. But I was sure that one day I would go home, even if no one ever said anything about it. It would come as a surprise, but a nice one this time.

She was always thinking about me, she was worried about my future. We would meet. What else was I looking for? I had answered her ungratefully and I didn't know how to find her to apologize. Some tears fell on Giuseppe's face, and he opened his eyes.

I was also sorry about the television. It would be a comfort to Adriana when I had gone to the upper school, as she called it. They had once been given a used one, but after a few months it broke and it wasn't possible to fix it or buy a new one. It had ended up in the garage shortly before I arrived. That winter we had watched all the episodes of *Sandokan* on the ground floor, sitting on the widow's couch. Nibbling on roasted chickpeas with her, we had wept for Marianna. The

Pearl of Labuan died in the powerful arms of the Tiger of Malaysia, whom we were mad about. But he had said that no woman would ever again have his love.

With an outburst of pride I had deprived Adriana of a pastime during my future absence. I reflected on it, a little mortified.

That day in June, caught between my two mothers. Every so often I think again of the hand of the first that for a few moments rested on my shoulder, at school. I still wonder why she placed it there, a woman so sparing of caresses.

28

A little more than a year had passed, but it was the longest year I had lived, and more than all the others would invade the future. I was too young, and propelled by the current, to see the river I'd been thrown into.

I went up different stairs with the same suitcase in one hand, the bag with the jumble of shoes in the other. My father drove in circles in search of a parking space, he wasn't experienced at driving in the city, and had apologized ahead of time, during the drive there, which otherwise passed in silence. He was indecisive at the intersections and other drivers honked repeatedly. Too saddened by my departure, I couldn't help. With one foot in the car and the other out, I had stood looking for a moment at Giuseppe, who cried and reached out his hands to me, while the mother held him. Go, go, she had said, over his cries, and so we had left each other. Adriana hadn't wanted to say goodbye, she was furious with me for breaking our vow not to be separated. She had hidden in the garage.

Somehow, we arrived at the address I had written down. The building was a couple of kilometers from the beach, and a few streets from the high school I would go to. As soon as I got out of the car I looked up at its severe and compact mass, at the light brown stucco. It was on the opposite side of the city from the house I had lived in until the year before. On the third floor a door awaited, slightly open. I stopped for a moment to calm my breath and my heart. I was about to knock when the door opened softly the rest of the way and in the shadowy light of the entry hall a gigantic girl appeared. So she seemed, compared to me. She greeted me with a broad, welcoming Hi, already full of familiarity. Her voice was enchanting: tiny bells rang inside it, fading a few seconds after the words.

"Come in, my mother will be back in a minute," she said, taking my bags.

I followed her into the room we would share. On the bed meant for me were two shoe boxes and new clothes for the school year. They were displayed in a certain order, like gifts for the bride in the days before a wedding. My future textbooks occupied a shelf of the bookcase that Sandra showed me, notebooks were ready on the desk, next to a calculator. Adalgisa had just come by, always generous.

"Your aunt came with all this stuff for you," Sandra confirmed.

She looked at me, her chestnut eyes surprised, maybe at my lack of enthusiasm for the gifts that had preceded me. And yet I needed them, the clothes she saw me in were shabby. But I was tired of receiving goods in that way.

I observed her as well, from head to toe, discreetly. In spite of her mass she seemed younger than seventeen, with skin as clear as a child's and the face of an enormous angel.

Her mother arrived with my father, whom she had met on the stairs. He didn't remember the last name of the family that was to host me and was wandering from one landing to the next, ringing at the doors. Signora Bice had rescued him from his difficulty and had drawn him on behind her, talking to him in the strong Tuscan accent she'd kept though she was far from her home. She led us into the kitchen and served cookies just taken from the oven, for my father a small glass of *vin santo* to dip them in.

"I pick this up when I go to see my other daughter in

Florence. Just taste it," and she waited for the comment after a sip. Then she turned to me, eating a cookie out of politeness, and assessed my appearance. "You're too skinny, look at us here!" She pointed to herself and her daughter and laughed, shaking her large bosom. Her prominent jaw and jutting lower front teeth gave her the air of a cheerful bulldog.

Signora Bice had guessed at first glance that the lack I suffered from did not concern food, I'm sure of it. In the years I spent with her she didn't offer herself as a substitute but confined herself to nourishing me with affection, admiring my commitment to studying, inventing the ritual of a chamomile tea after supper to induce sleep, which was always elusive. It was much more than what had been asked of her.

In the morning she came to wake us up, and found me with eyes open, often with a book in my hands. "Look at that lazybones," she said with a nod in the direction of her giant daughter asleep under the covers. We smiled conspiratorially, then she called her.

I'm still grateful to her, but after I graduated I didn't go back. I'm not in the habit of returning to those I've left.

That afternoon, before my father departed, I looked among the clothes displayed on the bed for something that Adriana could wear. They were too big for her, except for a hat and a scarf. *Don't be mad at me, Saturday I'll leave right after school, wait for me in the square at three*, I wrote in a note. I gave everything to him to bring to her.

"If you need to, go ahead and give her a slap, imagine she's your daughter," my father said to the signora, as he headed toward the door. He didn't know that he should use the formal "you." In his rough way he was asking her to love me like a mother; today I can believe that.

"Be careful Saturday when you get the bus to come home, it's not the only one that leaves from the city. Try to get the right one," he said, and then, again to the signora: "Maybe it's better if you can take her to the stop, at least the first time. Also to the school, please, she doesn't know where it is."

He spoke as if I were his. He had never concerned himself with me or the other children, really. Or maybe I just hadn't seen it. I lowered my head with emotion.

"Straighten your shoulders, or you'll be a hunchback."

The smack arrived strong and corrective. I remained with the imprint of my father's heavy palm on my back.

Later Sandra looked at my bewilderment.

"I'll help you unpack your bags," she offered.

"Would you mind if I stuck something on the wall?" I asked.

"No, of course not, here are the thumbtacks."

It was a drawing of my sister's that she had done on one of the rainy days that ended the summer. On the page she and I were holding hands amid flowering grasses. With my free hand I was holding a book that said "HISTORY" on the cover, while she held a sandwich. An edge of mortadella hung out, recognizable by the tiny white circles of fat amid the pink. She loved mortadella. Another difference caught by the pencil: she was smiling, showing some little teeth, but I wasn't. She's always been a genius, that Adriana.

I stared at the sheet of paper above the desk, and next to it I put up a kerchief she used to protect her head from the sun— I'd taken it unbeknownst to her, since she wouldn't need it anymore that year. Sometimes I'd seen her knotting it quickly behind her neck, when we went to pick fava beans, for instance.

"This thingy makes me sweat, but without it I get a bloody nose," she said.

While I pinned up the corners of the square of material I smelled the odor of Adriana's hair, and my discomfort diminished a little, like a fever. Then I had the kerchief near me every night, with its faded geometric motifs. Little houses, stylized bushes, baskets pulsed in the dark like phosphorescent figures roused by my eyes. Then I thought of her and the pact I had betrayed. One day I would be redeemed, if I could manage to bring her there with me. I had already estimated the measurements of the room, another bed could fit, and maybe Sandra and her mother and father, whom I had meanwhile met, wouldn't mind another guest. They'd laugh at Adriana's lightning-quick remarks, she would amaze them with her too adult common sense.

I already felt that I had to make up to her for some of the good luck I'd had, compared with her. And yet, of the two of us, I am the one who seems less fit for life.

What might happen to her while I wasn't there? My nights were filled by the disasters that could occur—after all, we had already lost a brother, and maybe that house attracted catastrophe. To her I devoted the wakefulness of that first period, but over the years I've always found something to agitate me, an excuse not to sleep. I still try different remedies, a new mattress, a drug just issued, a recently perfected technique for relaxation. I know already that I won't let myself yield to sleep, except for brief intervals. On the pillow every night the same knot of phantoms awaits me, the obscure terrors.

29

I got used to that house, too, and the family. Signor Giorgio, Sandra's father, was meek and silent. He was the only thin person in the family; by now his wife had given up trying to fatten him. On the other hand she did manage to increase my weight by a few kilos, like a good witch, one who wouldn't eat me. She served me generous portions and I finished them, embarrassed to leave anything on my plate.

Signora Bice took me to school the first day, as my father had asked her to. I learned the shortest route: halfway there some caged canaries on a balcony chirped—I would see them every morning.

"This is fine, thank you," I said to her when we arrived in sight of the pale yellow building and the groups of shouting boys and girls waiting to enter.

I went alone toward the open entrance. The lump in my throat of every beginning, of excitement and fear. In my class there was a girl I knew, who had gone to the same pool, years back. I was looking down and hadn't seen her; she called to me and we sat next to each other. She had recently moved to that neighborhood with her family.

"Why in the world are you enrolled in this high school, don't you live on the northern shore?" she asked later.

I opened my mouth to answer and closed it. I didn't know what to say, certainly not the truth, and at that moment no credible lie came to my aid.

"It's a long story," I murmured, just before the liberating

sound of the bell. I would tell her another time. Meanwhile I would prepare to lie.

Thus began years of shame. It wouldn't leave me, like an indelible stain, a birthmark on my cheek. I constructed a plausible story to explain to others, teachers, classmates, the absence of family around me. I repeated that my father the carabiniere had been transferred to Rome and I hadn't wanted to leave our city. I was staying with a relative and on the weekend I saw my parents, in the capital. The false turned out to be more plausible than what had really happened.

One afternoon Lorella, my deskmate, called to ask if she could borrow my mathematics notebook.

"I'll bring it over, where do you live, exactly?" I asked with excessive haste.

"No, I'm out with my mother, right in your street, what's the number?"

Now I was trapped, I had to tell her the number and floor. Only Signora Bice was home, luckily.

"A school friend is coming. She thinks you're my aunt, is that all right?"

"Of course, but remember to use the informal *you*," and she winked, perhaps with compassion. She understood, without need of explanations. She wanted to go to the door. "Come in, my niece is expecting you."

She also insisted on taking me to the bus stop, the first Saturday. The ride seemed interminable, and I was scared. Maybe in the town they'd already forgotten me. The time had been too short for attachment, even if we had been capable of it.

On Monday I had sent a card to my sister asking her to say hello to all the others for me. It would become a habit, I would send one every week, to remind my family that I was there and would come home. For Adriana and Giuseppe I drew hearts and wrote *smack*. Sometimes the mail was slow to arrive and I preceded it on the Saturday bus.

That first time I returned the road was blocked because of an accident a few kilometers from the town, and we were stopped for a long time. Surely my sister had gotten tired of waiting, even if she'd come to meet me. When the bus finally passed the "Welcome" sign, I was certain that she wouldn't be in the square and felt how difficult it would be to go home alone. But there she was, with her fists on her hips, elbows out, and on her face the expression of disappointment I knew. It was a few minutes before four.

"I can't wait hours for you. I also have things to do," she burst out.

She was really funny, in the still warm air she was wearing the wool hat I had given our father for her. In Adriana's theatrical language it meant that she had forgiven me the sin of leaving her. We crushed each other in a hug.

Maybe only she and I had seen in my return to the city a new separation. At home, our mother acted as if I had gone out for five minutes to buy salt at the tobacco shop. But she had kept a plate of pasta from lunch in the oven for me. She warmed it up, while I was in the bathroom. She must have calculated that between school and the bus I hadn't had time to eat.

"Here she is again," Sergio greeted me, with a mean look.

Nothing was different after a week.

One Friday in December I had a fever, and on Saturday Signora Bice was adamant, I couldn't go. I telephoned Ernesto's wine shop to ask him to tell my family, he said all right, but I had no idea if he'd understood, I heard the raised voices of the customers, the clink of the unbreakable glasses. Above all I didn't want Adriana to wait for me at the bus stop. I counted the days until Christmas vacation and then I crossed them off one by one as they passed.

When I got back I found her thinner and at war with everyone. She barely nodded even to me when I entered with my bag, and right afterward she went to the widow's, taking her bad mood down the stairs. Someone else had to tell me what was happening.

"What's wrong with her?" I asked my mother, who was standing at the kitchen table. Next to her, on the floor, a bucket of potatoes to peel.

"Who, your sister? She's gone mad, she won't eat. Only an egg beaten with marsala, early in the morning, but no one can see her, or she'll leave it. I make it and go back to my room."

"Why's she acting like that?" I asked, eating turnip greens and beans she'd set aside for me. I was sitting opposite her, with the plate on the bare surface of the table.

"She doesn't want to stay here anymore, that feral cat. She wants to go to the city with you," and, incredulous, she moved the knife through the air. "Sometimes she digs in her heels like a mule and won't go to school, that girl's not even scared of her father's beatings."

She shook her head, dropping a peel in the shape of a spiral on the floor.

"I've finished, I'll go down and call her," I said.

"See if she'll talk to you, she pays some attention to you. Your father's worried, he's afraid that child will die, too. He comes home every night with a fresh egg, he gets it from someone who works at the brick factory and has some land."

I went down to find my sister. She was on the couch and as soon as she heard me she grabbed the first magazine within reach and pretended to be absorbed in reading it. On the low table was a tray of cookies, but it seemed that not even one was gone. The widow tried, my mother had warned her. Adriana was not the type to fall for it.

I sat down next to her, we were at home there. I ate a cookie and then another, hoping it would be contagious. Once the civilities were over—how I had grown and how pretty I'd become—Maria busied herself in the kitchen. She opened the oven, we knew by heart the way the door creaked. The smell of meatloaf reached us. Adriana kept her eyes on the page of the magazine, her neck tense.

"What's the story?" I asked, breathing in her ear.

"A photo romance, can't you see?" she said, deliberately misunderstanding, in a slightly strident voice that seemed close to dissolving into tears.

"Not that. You, what's going on?"

"I don't know what you're talking about," she said, still without turning.

She crossed her legs and leaned her chest forward slightly to increase the distance from me, letting the magazine slide over in the other direction. Some pages fell closed, and she resumed reading randomly, too eagerly.

"I hear you don't eat, you go to school on alternate days. Upstairs they're worried about you."

"Worried, them, come on! They don't worry even if you die." And she turned some pages with an impetuousness that almost tore them.

"Can I help you?"

She didn't answer right away. I took her spindly arm with my hand and held it. I couldn't see her face, but I felt her resistance giving way a little at a time.

"When it's time I'll tell you," and she closed the magazine suddenly. "Bye, Mar'." She said goodbye as she rose, and I followed her. Maria came from the kitchen, she looked at me and pressed her lips together in a sign of impotence and apprehension. Adriana was already going up the stairs.

We had dinner without her, she retreated to the bedroom. Giuseppe was all over me constantly, as soon as I got home. I put him to bed and then went to her. I don't remember where the other boys spent the night, or the reason. My sister was sitting on the edge of the upper bunk, swinging her legs in the emptiness. She stopped while I climbed the ladder.

"That jerk Sergio broke it," she said, seeing that I noticed a missing step. "I don't want to stay here anymore," she began calmly, even before I settled myself next to her.

She started peeling the dark scab of a wound from the back of her left hand.

"Since you went back to the city, I've felt lost here. I'm always thinking about you and Vincenzo," and she pointed with her chin to the empty bed that no one had had the courage to take away.

She used her teeth for a second when she couldn't manage with her nails. Underneath appeared the new skin, bright pink, with the wish to yield to the pressure of the blood that permeated it.

"You have to let me come where you are, ask that lady who's so nice," she added, as if nothing were easier.

"How do you know she's nice? Plus there's no room there, her daughter and I are already crowded," I said, suddenly harsh.

"But I don't take up space. I can sleep with you, head to toe, remember when you came?" she asked, looking at me with the hopeful eyes of a begging child.

Of course I remembered, and yet I felt a resistance inside, and I didn't understand where it was coming from. I had often imagined taking her away with me. I leaned my back against the partition behind us, which divided the room from our parents'.

"Even if they said yes, who would give them the money to pay for your room and board?" and I beat my knuckles softly against the wall.

"They certainly don't have it," Adriana said quickly. And then, in a firm and thoughtful tone: "But there's someone who does. Adalgisa. You could try."

I straightened my back suddenly. "How can you think that? You're really crazy. I don't even know where to find her."

"All right, then. Here I don't feel like eating anymore. If I starve to death don't start crying afterward." She started swinging her legs again, unhurriedly, staring at the wall opposite. She had an advantage over me, a kind of plan already made in her mind. She played her hand like an adult.

"Come on, try to be reasonable. She already pays for my studies. What reason would she have to be concerned with you, too? You're not her daughter," I said, sweating.

"Neither are you, for that matter. Adalgisa took you just for a few years and then she sent you back."

"Yes, because she was sick and couldn't take care of me. She wanted to protect me."

If Adriana had looked at me, maybe she would have stopped, but her eyes were fixed on that dirty white wall in front of her and didn't see the desperation.

"Sick, come on! You still believe in fairy tales. She was pregnant, so she threw up. Is it possible you didn't think of that?"

"You're completely stupid," I said shaking my head. "She's sterile, that's why she adopted me."

"Seems to me it's her husband who couldn't, she has a baby now, and it's not the carabiniere's. That's why this disaster happened."

"What do you know about it? You're just an ignorant gossip"—and I turned away in disgust, panting. My heart was pounding furiously in my temples, like the fists of an imprisoned devil.

"Everybody knows. I heard Mamma and Papa, they were sorry that the baby's already getting big and they still haven't gone to give him a baptism present."

So Adriana pinned me to the truth, the night before Christmas Eve of 1976. At the holiday lunch there were two of us who didn't eat, the *brodo di cardo con stracciatella* would be left over for a snowy Santo Stefano.

I had no words to answer her, on the upper bunk of the bed that Adalgisa had sent us the year before. I grabbed her left hand and dug my nails into the flesh as hard as possible, reopening the cut. Together we watched the blood surfacing around the wounds of the only weapons that remained to me. She didn't cry and didn't move. When I took my fingers away, I hit her on the back to push her off, but she knew how to fall from up there. I cried with a violence I'd never felt before.

Then I lay down and didn't move. My body throbbed, breathing on its own. Adriana understood that she shouldn't climb back, she curled up down below, a short distance from my hatred.

30

The strange cry in the background when Adalgisa phoned me at Ernesto's wine shop. That's what it was: the wail of a child. Of the child. And the male voice that summoned her—maybe she had said he's awake—deeper than the one I knew. Is it Papa, I had asked her, and she: No, it's the television. Oh, the television.

The bed rest, the nausea of the first months of pregnancy, not of illness. Sudden tears—I thought they were for me—in the last weeks I'd spent with them, the angry tones one evening, behind the closed door of the bedroom. The ringing of the telephone followed by silence if I was the one who answered. Then that anxious rush to go out, usually to the pharmacy or the doctor. I'll go and get the medicine, Mamma, give me the prescription. No, I'm all right now, a little air will do me good. But one day the doctor's clinic was closed, and I had happened to see her strolling in that neighborhood. And later she had returned from there.

On the bus that was too slow I was reconstructing yet again the hints I'd ignored; they were always the same, but then every so often a new one came to mind. Her package of sanitary napkins in the bathroom that was always half full. And, back in time, her commitments at the parish church that became almost daily—I was older and could stay home by myself. Adalgisa was a catechism teacher. She listened to children reciting the Credo from memory, drumming with her fingers on the prayer book: that's what I saw when she used to take me with her.

*

I would return to the city before the end of the winter vaca-tion, with the excuse of homework to be done in a notebook that had been left at Signora Bice's. But actually I had some-thing urgent to ask her. And then I couldn't bear another day in the house where Adriana had said: Everybody knows. I wanted to die of shame, that night. My adoptive mother had sent me back because she was having a real child, everybody knew except me.

In the darkest hours after the news I tried to make my heart stop, it would take so little. Just keep it passive, as if under-water. I counted in silence, waiting for the oxygen that was left to dissolve into the bloodstream, for sleep to swallow me, heavier and heavier until it was transformed into death. But reaching the limit I breathed deeply, with a long hiss, I was the swimmer who emerged and filled her lungs with air to survive. The world I had known collapsed around me, pieces of sky fell on me like light pieces of scenery.

When dawn appeared at the window on the morning of Christmas Eve, my father woke on the other side of the wall. Rhythmic creaking of the slack old box spring. That hadn't been heard since the death of Vincenzo.

My mother in the kitchen, afterward. I was already there, in the dim light. She didn't see me right away, she was startled by a movement.

"Why didn't you tell me she was having a baby?"

She widened her arms and sat down, slowly shaking her head, as if she had expected the question for a long time and still didn't know the answer.

"She wanted to tell you, but time passed and she never showed up."

"Who's the father?"

"I don't know. It was the husband who couldn't have chil-dren, the other man got her pregnant without any fuss."

"It must be someone who goes to the church, she spent whole afternoons there," I thought aloud. I sat down, too. I rested one arm on the table beside me.

"As long as it wasn't the priest," my mother tried to joke. "I'm making coffee, you want a drop? Now you're grown," and she got up. She fussed with the coffeepot and the spoon, I didn't look at her. After a few minutes the gurgling and the aroma in the air. I grabbed her wrist as she was putting the cup for me down on the formica counter, and the little coffee I would have been allowed to drink spilled.

"Why didn't you tell me?"

She wasn't angry about the coffee, she let it spread, fragrant and hot, to the edge. One drop fell, another. She had already put in the sugar, I could tell from the smell. I went on squeezing her wrist, the skin whitened around the grip of my fingers.

"I was waiting till you were a little older, before causing you that pain."

I relaxed my grip and pushed away her arm.

"Where are they?" I asked.

"Who?"

"Adalgisa, the child."

"I don't know where she is with the baby, that's why I haven't gone to give her a present."

With the sponge she dried the table, the drops on the floor.

"Now don't be like that other girl, who's not eating. I'll beat you an egg, too, I have a lot for Christmas."

I left before she could try.

Adriana and I didn't speak to each other in the following days, but I felt her guilty, attentive gaze on me. She seldom went to the widow's, she was always around, at the proper distance. I was reading in bed one night and the book fell out of my hands. She was quicker than me, she came down the ladder like a cat and picked it up.

"Is it good?" she asked, opening it.

"I think so, I'm just at the beginning."

She knelt on the floor, she leafed through some pages. "Damn, not even a drawing. Will you lend it to me when you finish? Now that I've gotten to middle school I have to start reading some novels."

"O.K.," I said, and she climbed back up all excited.

She had suspended her hunger strike and I, too, made an effort, though the food tasted as bitter as medicine. I ate as little as possible so as not to attract attention.

I put the book on Adriana's pillow before I left. I couldn't find her in the house and it was already late, I went away without saying goodbye to her. Just beyond the big square I recognized her steps behind me, she reached me out of breath.

"Maria is like glue, she calls me every second. This time I ran away, she wanted help moving the furniture." She took a handle of the bag I was carrying, to share the weight. We walked toward the bus stop, and it was almost like holding hands.

"I talk too much sometimes," she admitted, panting from the uphill slope.

"There's nothing wrong with that if you tell the truth. It's the truth that's wrong."

On the steps of the bus I turned to look at her. "I'll ask the signora if she can make room for you. She's nice, you're right."

That wasn't the most urgent question burning in my mouth when Signor Giorgio opened the door. I had already forgotten Adriana, at least for a while. He was alone in the house, his wife and daughter were at the hospital. Sandra had broken a leg, without falling: I imagined the crack of bone under her weight. They would release her the next day, meanwhile for that night the mother would stay with her and I would have to wait to talk to her. I called Patrizia and she invited me to dinner at their house; we had seen each other at irregular intervals since I returned to school in the city.

Just as I was at the door putting on my coat Signora Bice turned her key in the lock. She was in a hurry, she had come to pick up something. I asked her about Sandra out of politeness but didn't even listen to the answer, it didn't much matter to me.

"I lost my aunt's phone number, could you give it to me?"

She seemed a little surprised, perhaps recalling my reticence whenever she mentioned Adalgisa. I hadn't understood what she knew about me, certainly that that aunt paid for my school.

"I had one, but then it changed and she forgot to write down the new one. I'm sorry."

"Then how do you manage . . . about the money?" I ventured without looking at her.

She held back a moment, maybe she was wondering if she could say it or not. "She comes by to settle the last Friday of every month."

Certainly in the morning, when I wasn't home. Otherwise we would have met.

"By herself?" escaped me.

"Yes. Now I must hurry, Sandra is waiting for me." Instead she took two steps in the direction of the bathroom and stopped. I stood there, hand on the front door. "You've come back early from the vacation and with a dark face. I'm glad you're going to your friend's, so you'll have a little fun. If you want to stay overnight you have my permission."

31

A slice of panettone in front of me, on the table covered by a Christmas-print tablecloth. Along the border a line of reindeer pulled sleighs piled with gifts, but the first was decapitated by the edge of the fabric, and the others appeared to be following him toward the same fate.

"You don't even like the candied fruit?" Patrizia's mother asked, since I wasn't eating.

Somehow released by her words, tears escaped, onto the candied fruit and the raisins, onto the soft yellow cake. At a nod from Vanda, her husband went into the living room and turned on the television. Motionless and tense on the chair next to mine, Pat looked at her mother. Apart from some attempts at conversation by Nicola that came to nothing, the dinner had been unusually silent. The scrape of silverware on plates, nothing more. They were sad because of the death of their old cat.

"She wasn't sick. She was pregnant," and I dried my cheeks with the red napkin. "I should have realized it right away, before they sent me back to the town."

"You weren't ready then." Vanda moved around the table, toward me.

"That's why they sent me back. But what did I have to do with it? I would have helped her, with the baby."

"Did she tell you?"

"I found out from my sister."

Vanda put a hand on my shoulder, in disbelief, and I leaned

my head against her soft wool hip. She held me lightly. I closed my eyes in weariness, I would have liked her to be silent and still, at least for a short while, so that I would have a few moments of rest, leaning on a human body, lost in its perfume, in a brief period of forgetting.

"That a child had to tell you, that's not possible. I was convinced that Adalgisa would speak to you, sooner or later—it was up to her to explain to you."

Her disdain vibrated deeply against my ear. I sat up, as if shocked.

"But now I know when she goes to pay the signora, in the morning, when I'm at school. The next time she'll find me."

Nicola called Vanda, she had to answer an urgent phone call.

"I'll be there, too, with you, I'll stay home from school," Pat offered. She had been silent the whole time.

"No. By myself."

"Anyway, I ran into her once—Adalgisa, with the baby and her man now," Patrizia resumed, as if she had suddenly recovered the memory. "You remember the widower who spent a lot of time at the church for a while, that handsome muscular guy?"

I didn't care about him, I barely remembered him. He had been married in our church and after the loss of his wife he came there some afternoons.

I argued a little with Pat—but with a sort of resignation that was now habitual—who had kept everything to herself until that moment. Even she.

"And the baby?" I asked, after the silence that followed.

"Who looked at him? I was too busy examining the father. And then he was sleeping."

At least she had seen who was holding him? That yes, Adalgisa. He wasn't even a stepbrother for me, I reflected. His mother wasn't mine.

Patrizia wanted to drag me into the gossip, but the subject was too painful. Vanda, coming back into the room, caught her last remark.

"Be quiet," she said, with a harsh look.

Later Pat asked me to go with her to a party the following week. I had no desire to, and she couldn't understand why. We were sitting opposite one another, legs crossed, on the Indian rug in her room. From the night table, the light of the lamp with its multicolored glass shade. She listed the boys we knew who would certainly be there and showed me her first pair of high heels, which she had bought in a store in the city center. I could wear a pair of her mother's, she insisted, we wore the same size. Vanda passed at that moment to say goodnight, and Patrizia asked her to intervene, to try to convince me. I repeated that I wasn't interested in parties.

"You have nothing to be ashamed of, you didn't choose what happened to you. It's the adults who are responsible." She said just that, her index finger pointing up like a warning.

"Well, thanks. But I wouldn't last in a crowd of kids having fun, I don't feel the same as other people anymore. I thought I was, but it was all false. Now I know, I have a different fate." I was talking to Vanda, as if Patrizia weren't there facing me, on the rug.

"Fate is a word for old people, you can't believe in it at fourteen. And if you do, you'd better change. It's true you're not like other people: no one has your strength. After what happened, you're still on your feet, clean and orderly, with an average of eight in your first semester. We admire you," she said, looking at her daughter for a moment as if in search of a confirmation taken for granted.

"You can't imagine how much effort it costs me to stay clean and orderly, as you say, and to study."

She sat on the bed with a sigh. "I know, but keep it up, don't let yourself be distracted by ugly thoughts."

Pattrizia grabbed my wrists, she squeezed them.

"You're my friend, between us it's the same as before."

"Between us, yes," and I bowed my head forward until our heads bumped with a very faint noise.

Down in the street there was a salvo of fireworks in anticipation of Epiphany.

32

I undressed in the dim light of the nearest street lamps. The cloudless sky had an unusually bright glow that hung over the city. On Signora Bice's balcony the chaise longue was still open from the previous summer, and I leaned against the backrest while I took off pajama top and bottom, socks, undershirt still warm from my body. Pale reflection of the stars on my breast. I had left Sandra in the room dreaming, her leg in the cast like a pillar under the covers.

The cold gripped me, as I'd hoped. It just needed time. I shivered and trembled, my teeth chattering. I had decided to sit there, naked, for half an hour, I would check the minutes with the alarm clock I'd brought with me. I held it in my hand for a while, observing the almost imperceptible movement of the phosphorescent minute hand, then I put it on the floor and sat on the chaise. I felt my nipples contract painfully, while my toes, farther from the heart, slept as if dead. With my eyes on the luminous figures and the pale green line that moved so slowly, I resisted going over again what I would say the next day. It was the night between the last Thursday and Friday of January, I had to get myself a fever for the morning.

A little before eight the silhouette of Signora Bice, who hadn't seen me leave the room, appeared behind the opaque glass of the door, but I was already sick. She heard me coughing and looked for the thermometer in her daughter's night table. I had a fever, above a hundred.

"Then stay home. I'll bring you breakfast," and she took a

few steps in the direction of the kitchen. She stopped, arrested by a sudden thought. She looked at me.

I stayed in bed with a book, but I couldn't get past the first page. I would read a few lines and they left no trace, I had to keep starting over with the same paragraph. I waited for the sound of the bell. The first time it was only the mailman, with something to sign. Attempts at conversation by Sandra, after she woke up, fell into the void of the hours. At eleven it was Adalgisa. As she was coming up the stairs, Signora Bice stuck her head in the room, with a questioning expression.

"I have to talk to her," I said.

"All right, as soon as we've settled our business I'll call you," and she closed the door.

The footsteps arriving and then in the entrance, muffled, the click of the lock behind the woman who had brought me up. The voices greeting each other, Adalgisa still ignorant that I was straining to hear. They went into the kitchen, maybe for coffee. After a few minutes a sound of chairs moving; I was afraid she would elude me, again. I didn't wait to be called.

Her look when she saw me is one of the most vivid memories I have of her and probably the most damaging. She had the eyes of someone who is caught in a trap and finds no way out, as if a ghost had re-emerged from a buried time, to pursue her. It was me, barely more than a child, and children don't inspire fear.

She remained seated, tilted a little to one side after a slight sudden movement of her chest. The broad mole on her chin seemed darker, perhaps an effect of the pallor around it. She had shaved the hairs that grew on it, they just barely emerged from the surface. The money she paid for me every month stood out on the brown wood, beside the sugar bowl.

"You're not at school?" she articulated, with difficulty moving lips painted a brighter red than usual.

I didn't answer. I was burning, and I stayed on my feet, with the help of the wall.

"She has a fever," Signora Bice intervened. "She wants to talk to you, come into the dining room, no one will disturb you there."

She led us in, Adalgisa went ahead of me and seemed unsteady on the heels of her suede shoes. Her figure had softened into more feminine curves, I watched her moving in the hall in a sort of milky haze. We sat at the rectangular table in the room that was almost never used, as Signora Bice wished. Then she went out and we were alone with the silence, facing each other. Her green wool dress was tight under the pressure of her bosom, which had grown larger.

I looked at her now in no hurry, I felt strong thanks to the wrong I'd suffered. And furious, but also calm, after all that time. I'd been waiting a year and a half for her, it was up to her to begin.

She brought her hands from her lap to the table. Her fingers were bare, she wasn't wearing a wedding ring. I thought of the child, wondering who was taking care of him right now; noon was approaching and she wasn't on the way home. A sigh lifted the *presentosa* that hung on her chest, making it flash.

"I loved you and I love you now, too," she began.

"I don't care anymore about your love, it's obvious how much you wanted me. Tell me why you sent me away."

"It wasn't easy. I don't know what ideas you had about . . . " and she traced the carved edge of the wooden table with her index finger.

"What ideas should I have had? All you told me was the lie about the family that wanted me back—in the town they knew and didn't say. When I left, you were in bed throwing up, I thought you were seriously ill. *I* was worried about *you*. I called and no one answered, I went to our house twice and it was closed up. I thought you were far away, in a hospital, that you might die. And for months I waited for you, hoping you'd be better and would come and get me."

She dabbed at her tears with a handkerchief that she took from her purse, which was hanging on the back of the chair next to her.

"It wasn't easy," she repeated, shaking her head.

"You could have simply told me the truth," and I leaned toward her across the table.

"You were too young for the truth, I wanted to wait till you got a little older." She, too: like the other.

A fit of coughing, which hadn't dared to interrupt until then, gripped me and gave us a pause.

"Didn't you always preach that marriage is an indissoluble sacrament?"

"The child had to have his father nearby," she justified herself. "I understand your rage, but I wasn't alone in the decisions."

"I would have come with you, just to stay close to you."

I tried to control my voice and hold back my tears. Suddenly I felt every single degree of my body temperature and an irremediable weakness.

"I tried to arrange things in the best possible way. I didn't want to be separated from you, but that's what happened."

"Didn't your husband say anything? Couldn't he keep me with him?"

"It was a difficult moment for him. He didn't feel up to it."

She brought her hands back to her lap, her head lowered. I slumped against the chair back and stared at the cut-glass pendants of the chandelier, with their countless facets. They seemed to be quivering, as if there had been an earthquake, but it was only my fever.

"You didn't come to see me once, in fact you purposely avoided me."

"I was waiting for the right moment, I told you. I helped you from a distance."

I no longer remembered what I had imagined shouting at

her or it came out of my mouth without energy, as if it counted so little now. In the end what could I do to her? Even the pajama button that I had been twisting for several minutes, when it shot out toward her didn't hit her.

We were silent for a while. Her lips a thin double line of lipstick. Then she raised one finger slightly.

"I've stayed informed, you know. Don't think I don't feel responsible for you."

"Forget it," and I turned sideways, toward the print of old Florence on the wall. From the kitchen came the smell of the ragú that Signora Bice was making. Then the sound of keys and the front door opening and closing, Signor Giorgio was arriving for lunch.

"Are you happy now?" slipped out, somewhere between an accusation and a kind of curiosity.

She didn't answer, but after a few seconds she brightened and took her wallet out of her purse. Carefully she removed a photograph, smiled at it and put it on the table, pushing it toward me with satisfaction. I disobeyed the impulse to tear it up right in front of her, I felt superior to such a gesture. Without deigning to glance at it I turned the child over and pushed him back toward the mother, right up to the edge of the table. She caught him just before he fell.

The clatter of silverware in the other room, Signora Bice was setting the table. Adalgisa roused herself, she looked with a start at the small gold watch I'd always seen on her wrist. She got up, I didn't move. I didn't know much more than before.

"Just a minute, please, I need help for my sister Adriana. She can't stay in the town much longer."

"What class is she in?" she asked, trying to hide her impatience.

"First year of middle school."

"We'll talk about it next time, don't worry. Remember I'm here. And I urge you, continue to do well in school."

Quickly she wrote the new telephone number on a sheet of paper.

"If you need to, call."

She hesitated a moment longer, at the time I didn't understand why, since she was in such a hurry. Maybe she was wondering if it would be right to come close to me and how close, to say goodbye. My attitude must have discouraged her; she stayed on the other side of the table. I got up, too—my legs weak—and went to the window, as if she were no longer there. I looked outside, at the street and the balconies opposite faded by winter, the city bus that was taking the children home.

33

S tarting that Friday in January Adalgisa began to surprise me. I imagined that I wouldn't see her again for I
don't know how long, maybe forever. She would spend
money on me as usual, from a distance. Instead she telephoned two days later. Signora Bice answered, "She's here,"
looking at me deliberately. I pointed toward the bathroom
with a nod of urgency and shut myself in. Sitting on the edge
of the tub I heard them talking about me—my studies, meals,
the usual subjects. She called again later and I couldn't
escape.

"I thought of renewing the pool membership, we could go
together one of these afternoons."

"I'm not interested," I said immediately.

"Dancing class, then."

"Not that, either."

I used to like it a lot, she insisted, and I would see my
friends again.

"They've probably forgotten about me by now. And I'm
sorry, dinner's ready."

I didn't want more than what was necessary from her. But
the no to dancing class weighed on me at night like undigested
food. I really had liked it.

I found her outside school on a rainy day that had started
out clear. In the crush of parents who had come to get their
children, she was waiting with a big man's umbrella. I pulled
back, but was immediately shoved forward by the kids who

were swarming away. She was there just for me, already she was saying hello and I couldn't avoid her.

"I was sure you didn't have anything to keep the rain off. It was sunny this morning."

She offered me her arm and I ignored it, I walked beside her hoping that none of my classmates would notice us. I wouldn't have known how to say who she was.

At the same time I felt a kind of relief, a temptation to imagine that I was like everybody else, for once. Someone had come to get me, too, in the winter weather.

She talked about the car that was parked a little too far away, everyone had started out at the same time in that storm. Above us, water in torrents. There it was, washed by the rain, her blue SUV. She sheltered me while I got in the car and went around to get in the driver's seat. A slightly sour smell lingered inside, from when she'd spilled a bottle of vinegar, years earlier. But I was hit more powerfully by her perfume, as soon as she turned her head. In the morning she bathed the hollow behind her ear and her wrists, I knew by heart those gestures at the mirror.

On the dashboard was a shiny San Gabriele magnet, with a small color photograph of the baby and the legend "Don't hurry, think of me." Next to it was the old one with my face, faded, in black and white. I looked at the drops dripping down the fogged-up glass and was silent until we arrived.

"Here's some beef with tomato sauce that I made today, you can warm it up," she said at the door, handing me a pot wrapped in a napkin.

I stopped for a few minutes on the stairs. What was happening? Why was Adalgisa unexpectedly so available? It frightened me, confused me. I'd given up on her, lost faith. But suddenly, after the meeting I had forced on her, she appeared so kind. I felt the danger of yielding to her again. And the inexpressible desire.

For several weeks I heard nothing more. She seemed to have disappeared again. The pot that had contained the meat waited for her on a shelf in Signora Bice's kitchen, washed and dried. Had my sullen behavior driven her away? No, it was only the start of her erratic appearances. In time I got used to her being there and disappearing every so often, for longer or shorter periods. She divided her time between me and her new family. I waited for her without admitting it. I acted a little offended when she came back. It was always like that, at least as long as my need for her lasted.

I didn't care about her visits, I was convinced of it, but I started at the sound of the bell.

She showed up with a sweater in my favorite color, I took it from her with a movement that was too abrupt.

"I got red. Is the size right?"

I shrugged and went to put it away without even trying it on. She followed me into the bedroom. She looked around.

"You're a little tight here," she said thoughtfully. She told me she was moving, that was why she'd disappeared. "I'm sorry you haven't seen me, I've had a million things on my mind." She had returned to the house by the sea.

"Everything has to be put away. With Guido always gone for work and a small child it will take months."

I'd never heard her say the name of the man who had changed our lives. She smiled at the name of her child: Francesco, like one of the saints she prayed to. I listened attentively even though I had turned away so that she couldn't see.

"Your bed is still there," she murmured, more to herself, fingering the Abruzzese blanket that kept me warm at night.

In her bag she had other things for me: knee socks, a silver bracelet, a stick of cocoa butter for my chapped lips. I accepted it all without embarrassment, without thanking her. While she put the things on the night table I was deciding what to bring to my sister.

"Sunday will you come to lunch with us?" she asked suddenly.

"Weekends I go back to the town," I answered after a pause, without looking at her.

"Maybe the next one," she proposed.

Many Sundays passed.

During the Easter vacation I told my mother about the invitation, in one of those moments of intimacy that occurred when we were alone in the kitchen. I was helping her peel hard-boiled eggs that the priest would bless.

"Accept. Remember that Adalgisa raised you."

It wasn't her only attempt at reconciliation over the years. She felt toward her cousin a kind of joyless gratitude for having brought me up so differently from her other children.

"If not for her, instead of going to school now you'd be laboring in the countryside. You haven't known poverty, poverty is more than hunger," she said to me one day, as a warning. And then: "She was wrong, but you can't sulk about it your whole life."

Adalgisa stopped talking about the lunch, but I felt that it was an obsession. We continued to see each other at Signora Bice's, except once when she persuaded me to go with her to the department store. She was in the mood to spend, she bought things for me, for the baby. As we wandered from one department to another we really might seem mother and daughter again.

She tried again in early May. She came upstairs excited and warm, with a strange restlessness.

"Guido would really like to meet you now," she said, repeatedly joining her hands, as if in a sort of slow, silent applause. "Don't answer me no right away, I'll call you Friday."

Signora Bice looked at us with an encouraging smile. On

Friday she handed me the phone, but first she covered the receiver.

"Go, it's really important to her."

So, to my surprise, I found myself dressing carefully that Sunday morning, making my eyes look bigger with Sandra's eyeliner and mascara, maybe overdoing it a little. Adalgisa telephoned early, impatient to come and get me. I said I'd rather walk, it was so sunny.

I wasn't satisfied, at the last minute I changed my clothes. I added color to my pale cheekbones. I didn't even understand who I was getting ready for. I was late getting to the bus stop. Adriana had already arrived and was waiting with a scowl.

"Are you crazy leaving me alone in the middle of the city? You call me at Ernesto's phone booth, you make me get up early, and then you're not here?"

I had asked her to come with me, I didn't want to go alone. For a moment I regretted it. Her clothes were too small, her shoes dirty. Her hair as greasy as ever, even though it was Sunday, bath day. She caught my look.

"If I'd washed it I would have missed the pullman."

"Bus, Adriana, you have to say you came on the bus and hadn't told me." I hugged her.

We spit in turn on a Kleenex and cleaned the old loafers, laughing a little. We set off quickly, chatting, I had so many instructions for her.

"Speak in Italian, please. Except for the bread don't eat with your fingers, use the silverware. And chew with your mouth closed, don't smack your tongue."

"Oh Lord, how nervous you're making me. You'd think we're going to see the Queen of England. Have you completely forgotten now what she did to you?"

"Don't stick your nose in. Behave nicely if you want Adalgisa to help you come to the city."

We still had a long way to go, but at the bus and tram stops Adriana insisted that she wanted to keep walking.

We arrived late. I rang at the garden gate, the trill was new, more melodious. They had also replaced the fence, so you couldn't see anything from outside. A last look at Adriana's sweaty face, I arranged her hair behind her ears, maybe like that it was less noticeably dirty.

"Be careful," I repeated.

The click of the lock, and we entered. Fleetingly glimpsed, the grass freshly cut, different flowers in the flower beds, arranged in a geometric order. A bush just planted, the earth newly turned. My mouth dry and a tumult of feelings in my chest. The man in the doorway, in a white shirt.

"We were expecting one young lady and two came," he said, smiling in a friendly way. He shook our hands, as if we were adults, with a vigorous, pleasant gesture.

"Hello. My sister surprised me," I said, in explanation.

"Good, come in. We'll add a place."

We stood still, close together, in the dining room, intimidated. In appearance the house was the same as before, but something indefinable seemed irreparably changed.

"Adalgisa will be here in a moment, she's with the baby. He eats at twelve on the dot and at this time he should be sleeping. Meanwhile you can wash your hands, the bathroom's there."

"I know, thanks."

Squeezing her legs together Adriana rushed to the door, opened it noisily. She had already wet her pants, and I had forgotten. While I closed the door I noticed the look that followed us.

"I have a few drops in my underpants, let's hope no one can smell it."

I reassured her, not me. She stood mesmerized before the

makeup shelf, but I snapped her out of it. Without a watch I'd lost any sense of time; it seemed very late for lunch.

No one was in the living room. Two voices in the kitchen, instead, and the smell of fish the way Adalgisa prepared it. The impulse to go in, to nose around the stove, taste this or that, remained from my previous life. One step and I stopped, confused. The house no longer belonged to me. I was a guest.

I wanted to see my room, though, even just for a second.

"Adriana, I'll show you where I used to sleep, it's this room here on the side."

My bed was still there, it was true. But my books, my stuffed animals, the Barbies I'd played with until middle school had vanished. The shelves were occupied by ships in bottles of all sizes—some were tiny, with sails like postage stamps. One, under construction, was sitting on the desk: it was already in the bottle, but the masts were bent over the bridge and there were some threads long enough to reach the wooden surface of the desk. Around it were the tools: tweezers, a case of gouges, other tiny implements used for something or other, who knows what.

There was nothing left of me there.

"Do you like it?"

I started, but the question was for Adriana. I had lost sight of her, she was holding a bottle in her too curious hands.

"It was one of the most difficult to assemble," he said, approaching to explain the mystery.

"You're so clever, it came out really beautifully," she complimented.

"You should use the formal *you*," I whispered, not softly enough.

"No, leave her alone, she's so spontaneous."

Adalgisa arrived, finally.

She was wearing a blue dress, with an apron tied over it. No surprise at seeing Adriana, she greeted her kindly, asked about our parents. She took my hand, hers damp with emotion.

"Guido, I've talked about her so much and now here she is with us. You've already introduced yourselves, haven't you?"

"Of course. You're right, she's really a smart girl."

Then she hugged me tighter, and a thank you escaped her, followed by a small movement, almost a childish hop of joy.

She led us to the table and added a place for Adriana. When my sister saw her lining up the silverware for dessert in front of the gilt-edged plate, she blurted out:

"What do I do with all these? Fork and knife's good for me, a spoon if the soup is thin."

I stepped on her foot secretly, I sat next to her to control her. He sat opposite, he looked at her in amusement.

"Don't worry, use the ones you want. But you'll see that the smallest will be useful for something good, later."

Then he asked her if she liked school and Adriana answered so-so.

"I know how clever you are, Adalgisa is always talking about it," he said to me, as if to apologize for his interest in my sister.

They talked about the town, where he'd gone as a child to visit relatives. He remembered endless lunches, delicious sausages. In return she described Half-Cigar's sausages, which would wake the dead. She felt really comfortable with him, my warnings forgotten. I trembled every time she opened her mouth. Adalgisa went back and forth to the kitchen, content.

Fish antipasto. She observed her companion's first bite to see how it was. He approved with a nod. Adriana examined a shrimp without its shell, turning it on her fork.

"Is something wrong?" Guido asked.

"It looks like a worm," and then she tasted it happily.

They began joking about peoples who eat insects and worms. I was hot, and not very hungry. By now I had stopped pressing Adriana's foot at every inopportune remark. She was herself.

Adalgisa served spaghetti with clams, spattering oil on Guido's shirt.

"I'm sorry, dear, I'll get the talcum powder right away."

She applied it to the stain with devoted hands, he leaned back, to make it easier. A slow caress, across his chest, before leaving him and going back to her seat. I'd never seen her like that with her husband.

"No grains of sand this time?" she asked then, slightly apprehensive.

"It's really delicious," Adriana mumbled, chewing, but the question wasn't for us.

"No sand, no, I don't think so, not so far. Only a little salty, but that doesn't matter. The clams should soak longer."

Suddenly, from the other room, a small voice called mamma.

"He woke up early. Now you'll see him," Adalgisa said, getting up.

"No, dear, stay and eat. Francesco has to obey the rules."

"But he's starting to cry," she protested weakly.

"We've made rules, in agreement with the doctor. It doesn't matter if he cries, he'll fall asleep again soon." He pointed to her plate and: "Go on, it's getting cold."

She sat down again, but on the edge of the chair, her back rigid. She twirled the spaghetti on her fork and left it there, holding the handle with inert fingers. The child's crying alternated with pauses in which Adalgisa's face cleared. Then she would almost raise that fork as Guido had asked. But the wail resumed, gradually louder.

He took a swallow of white wine from the crystal glass, dabbed his lips with the napkin.

"Don't keep doing that. If it's closed it should be thrown away." In the neutral tone there remained barely a trace of the playful kindness of before.

I turned to Adriana. She was forcing open a clam with the tip of her knife.

"I don't want to waste it," she said, putting it down on the clean plate.

The sound of the shell on the china was hidden by the child's voice, louder now. The father was drumming on the table with his right hand. At a certain point he got up and we all followed him with our eyes, sure he would go to his son's room. Instead he went into the kitchen: Adalgisa had forgotten the main course: sea bass baked with potatoes. She put her hands back in her lap, powerless.

"You'll go and get him now, won't you?" Adriana incited her, taking advantage of that brief absence.

She didn't answer, maybe she didn't even hear. He returned with the dish and placed it directly on the linen tablecloth. He removed the skin and the bones, served us generous helpings of white fish. Then the vegetable. He told us to eat, trying to come up with a smile. The cries vibrated in the air.

"Maybe he's sick," Adalgisa tried, pleading.

"In five minutes he's asleep. It's just willfulness."

Again he went to the kitchen and returned with the bread basket. He replaced the now cold spaghetti with the main course and she turned away slightly, she didn't even want to see that plate. Two deep furrows at the sides of her mouth suddenly aged her.

Adriana barely tasted it, no one else touched the food. Silence at the table, opposed to those cries from the other room. They diminished and ceased suddenly. Guido nodded, pleased. Then again, even louder.

At the time I couldn't explain how Adalgisa could resist those cries, I suffered for her. But it was her companion who with his gaze kept her still.

Adriana got up, and maybe they didn't even notice it. I had no doubt that she needed the bathroom. I was as if paralyzed in my chair, the cries filled house and minds. Maybe it was only minutes, but that interval of crying that had changed the day seemed interminable. Adalgisa slumped in her chair, her attention on the chandelier. The makeup over one eye smeared. He traced the gold border of the plate with his fingertip. Then I saw him start because of something behind me. I turned.

Adriana was holding the child, he had already calmed down. She was rocking him with light movements, his face still red and upset, tufts of hair pasted to his forehead by sweat.

"How dare you touch my son?" the father said, getting up suddenly. The chair overturned behind him. He was panting, a vein pulsing on his neck.

Adriana didn't even consider him. She gave the baby gently to his mother.

"He had his hand caught in the bars of the crib," and she pointed to the red marks on his tiny wrist, the swelling already visible on the skin. She pushed his hair back and dried the tears with a napkin before she sat down again next to me. Adalgisa kissed his sore little fingers one by one.

With the palm of my hand I felt my sister's hard, tense leg. She had been so strong, but she was trembling.

Guido picked up the chair and fell back in it, arms dangling to the floor. Nothing remained of the man who had raised his voice at a girl, pointing a threatening finger at her. He looked inadvertently at his two glasses, of water and wine. I don't know how long he sat like that, but it's the image I have of him from that day.

No one spoke. Only a hiccup every so often from the baby, who had gone back to sleep. I had simply to touch Adriana's shoulder, we understood each other.

"Thank you for lunch, it was all delicious, really. But we'd better go now, my sister has to catch the bus for the town in an hour," I said quickly. Adalgisa looked at us with impotent, sorrowful eyes. With an almost imperceptible movement she shook her head no. It wasn't how she had imagined that Sunday.

I went over to say goodbye to her and smelled the odor of warm bread that came from her son. Sometimes he jerked in his deepest sleep. I obeyed the impulse to touch him on his knitted cotton shirt. Maybe it was one of mine, so soft. Adalgisa had saved them in a box on the highest shelf in the closet, along with other memories of my childhood. Instinctively I removed a hair missed on the blue of her dress, as if to restore her to the perfection of that time.

"At least take some dessert," she ventured.

"Maybe the next time," Adriana said.

"One moment," said Guido. He wrapped a piece of cake in paper and accompanied us to the door.

"I'm fixing things up, out here. Come again, we'll eat outside."

I closed the gate behind us, we breathed deeply.

"You were great," I said.

"Someone had to go to that infant. Didn't they imagine he was screaming in pain?"

We set off along the sidewalk, skirting the garden. At the corner I changed my mind, it was early for the bus. I persuaded her to go down to the beach. Not many open umbrellas, the season had just begun. We took off our shoes and she followed me to the edge of the water, a little doubtful. We were almost in the same place as that long-ago day with Vincenzo. Silently we remembered him.

Adriana looked at me as if I were mad, then she, too, took off her clothes and left them on the warm sand, along with her fear. She trusted my hand and we went in, with our underwear on. A school of tiny fish brushed our ankles. Time to get used to the cold. She walked warily, I swam around her a little. I splashed her and in return she pushed my head under.

We stopped, facing each other, so alone and close, the water up to my chest and to her neck. My sister. Like an improbable flower, growing in a clump of earth stuck in the rock. From her I learned resistance. We look less like each other now, but we find the same meaning in this being thrown into the world. In our alliance we survived.

We looked at each other over the lightly tremulous surface, the dazzling reflections of the sun. Behind us the safe-water boundary. Squeezing my eyelids just a little I imprisoned her between the lashes.